THREADBARE

LEA ANN W. HALL

LifeRich
PUBLISHING

Copyright © 2016 Lea Ann W. Hall.

All rights reserved. No part of this book may be used or reproduced by any means, graphic, electronic, or mechanical, including photocopying, recording, taping or by any information storage retrieval system without the written permission of the author except in the case of brief quotations embodied in critical articles and reviews.

LifeRich Publishing is a registered trademark of
The Reader's Digest Association, Inc.

LifeRich Publishing books may be ordered
through booksellers or by contacting:

LifeRich Publishing
1663 Liberty Drive
Bloomington, IN 47403
www.liferichpublishing.com
1 (888) 238-8637

Because of the dynamic nature of the Internet, any web addresses or links contained in this book may have changed since publication and may no longer be valid. The views expressed in this work are solely those of the author and do not necessarily reflect the views of the publisher, and the publisher hereby disclaims any responsibility for them.

Any people depicted in stock imagery provided by Thinkstock are models, and such images are being used for illustrative purposes only. Certain stock imagery © Thinkstock.

ISBN: 978-1-4897-1031-4 (sc)
ISBN: 978-1-4897-1030-7 (e)

Library of Congress Control Number: 2016917747

Print information available on the last page.

LifeRich Publishing rev. date: 11/30/2016

*To my husband, H. L. Hall,
who made this book possible
in countless ways*

Acknowledgements

Thanks to LifeRich Publishing staff members (Erin Cole, Connie Stark, Adam Tinsley (and the text and design teams), and especially Jennifer Morris) who guided me along the road to getting this book published.

Table of Contents

Prologue xi

Chapter 1 1
Chapter 2 5
Chapter 3 9
Chapter 4 13
Chapter 5 15
Chapter 6 19
Chapter 7 25
Chapter 8 31
Chapter 9 35
Chapter 10 41
Chapter 11 47
Chapter 12 51
Chapter 13 55
Chapter 14 61
Chapter 15 65
Chapter 16 71
Chapter 17 75
Chapter 18 81
Chapter 19 87
Chapter 20 89
Chapter 21 95
Chapter 22 103

Chapter 23	107
Chapter 24	109
Chapter 25	115
Chapter 26	121
Chapter 27	125
Chapter 28	129
Chapter 29	133
Chapter 30	137
Chapter 31	139
Chapter 32	145
Chapter 33	151
Chapter 34	155
Chapter 35	159
Chapter 36	163
Chapter 37	171
Chapter 38	175
Chapter 39	181
Chapter 40	185

Prologue

After sunset, well after the last glimmer of sunlight had vanished from the remote asphalt road, a lone vehicle appeared and slowed. Its headlights winked out before it stopped, but its engine continued to idle. It might have been a van or a large car. It was impossible to tell.

The driver reached over and turned off the switch to the interior lights, then rolled out of the vehicle and quietly closed the door until it touched the latch. The outer darkness absorbed the car's shape and even its color. It appeared that the vehicle was a large sedan, purring a steady stream of cloudy exhaust fumes, which drifted away lazily on a cold, moisture-laden breeze.

For several seconds, the driver stood facing the closed door, peering above the rooftop, as though cautiously casing the scene. The head and shoulders were silhouetted almost indistinguishably above the car.

Then the driver's shadowy figure moved swiftly around the back of the car and opened the rear door on the far side. No interior lights glowed. The furtive shape had made sure of that.

The driver leaned inside the dark door for a few moments then began pulling something heavy out of the car. The bulky object was long enough to force its mover to struggle backwards halfway into the frosty drainage ditch before two legs finally dropped clear of the car, revealing the semblance of a human form.

The driver readjusted the awkward load, grasping under the armpits of the unwieldy body and dragging the dead weight with its lanky legs, along the roadside of the ditch, to about ten yards beyond the front of the car. There the driver wrestled the lifeless form into place, rolling it face down and positioning its length directly across the path of the idling car.

The driver straightened, studied the dark scene for a brief moment, then charged to the car's open back door and slammed it shut with a thud. The inky figure continued swiftly on around the rear of the car en route to the driver's door, thus avoiding the choice of going back around the front and having to encounter the crumpled body one more time.

Jumping into the car and whipping the door shut, the driver gritted his teeth and shifted into forward, lurching over the inert form, then floored the accelerator, roaring away from the devastation left behind by the tires.

Chapter 1

NEAR THE END of the twentieth century, suburban St. Louis is a nice place to live, where even the police lead pretty routine lives most of the time . . . most of the time.

St. Louis is a diversely populated area nestled along either bank of the Muddy Mississippi, midway on its course to the Gulf. Even at its halfway point, Ole Man River stretches wider than any other river in the United States. Half a dozen bridges straddle the huge, brown scar, stapling Missouri and Illinois precariously together.

Travelers driving west through the rundown Illinois side, approach the river on intertwining feeder routes of highways and interstates. Downtown St. Louis, Missouri, looms on the western riverbank. A scattering of skyscrapers forms a dignified background of mute homage to a shinning arc of beauty. The Gateway Arch stands alone and aloof from the riverfront activities bustling just below her deeply planted feet. Shimmering silver in her serene pose, her graceful heights of stunning simplicity dwarf the mighty buildings behind her.

She commands before her, a broad sweep of concrete steps, which the river had dared to attack just one time, before receding gradually to its normal tame flow, slowly relinquishing its wild desire to lap at her sturdy, triangular legs.

Some of the towns and subdivisions on the far western outskirts are modern and shiny in every respect, but the commute to downtown is long and congested. Other towns, not so far from the muddy river, have rich histories dating to pre-Civil War times and still boast their own main streets, where the old-timers can point out locations of former hotels, ice cream shops, and train depots that have become thriving boutiques, or other small enterprises.

A fair number of the pro athletes who play for St. Louis teams either keep their homes in St. Louis suburbia, even after they've been traded away; or they return to stay after their sports careers are over. It's a nice place to live . . . most of the time.

Phil Vincent, partner in a downtown law firm, managed to stand almost still beside the sleek, purring refrigerator, while his wife Beth hurriedly finished stitching his tie. As he watched Nan, his teenage daughter, pop a last corner of toast into her mouth and chase it with a final swig of orange juice, Phil smiled a little ruefully. Not only did she favor his looks, like being tall, but she also possessed many of his other traits, including his energy and haste, in an unlikely combination with orderliness. Shortening her name from Nancy to Nan when she was in third grade was indicative of her directness. She definitely was her father's daughter in all respects.

Sitting at the large, round table in the kitchen's sunny breakfast nook, Nan was wearing her fire-engine red, ski-style pajamas, gray gym socks, and a fleecy pale pink robe.

She had a sprinkling of tiny freckles across her cheeks and her dad's sparkling deep blue eyes. She hurried to the sink with her dishes, her heavy mane of straight auburn hair falling like a curtain across her perky profile as she loaded the dishwasher.

Glancing up, she caught her father's eye and wriggled her nose at him like a bunny. He returned the silent communication with a pleased chuckle. Trying not to disturb his wife's sewing, he moved one hand up to smooth back the lock of auburn hair drooping across his forehead.

Beth bit off the pink thread and said, "There, that ought to hold for now. So much for trying to be helpful." Earlier, she'd noted that her winsome husband looked great, as always, in a gray herringbone sport coat, starched white shirt, and charcoal slacks. However, his tie was askew, because the narrow end hadn't quite made it through the label on the back of the wider end. So as he'd bent his head to kiss Beth good-bye, she'd reached out to straighten his tie and caught the square-cut diamond of her wedding ring on the label, pulling it loose on one side. Thus, the quick fix.

Chapter 2

PHIL HAD MADE partner earlier than most attorneys, and his specialty was federal tax law. Because he always stayed focused, the work he produced was thorough and accurate. In short, his law firm considered him to be one of its essential resources.

Grabbing his thick burgundy briefcase, he strode across the kitchen toward the door leading into the garage. Usually at this point, he bounded through the door flinging a few words over his shoulder to the effect that he shouldn't be too late. But today, after opening the door wide, he swung around to announce, "Mark my words, my pretty gals. On this bright November day, a certain St. Louis lawyer, dedicated though he is to his profession, will return home to appear in this very doorway before the sun has set."

His wife smiled wryly, shaking her tousled dark pixie hair at Phil's poetic prose and rolling her cola brown eyes doubtfully at Nan, who displayed a skeptical expression of her own and muttered to the closing door, "Right, Dad. That'll be a first."

Beth, dressed in her daily house uniform of faded jeans and a sweatshirt (this one being navy), held up the needle and sighed, "I can't believe the only threaded needles in this house are pink, red and green. Any other time, I'd have black or white —or both, more likely."

"Chill out, Mom. You know Dad wouldn't have waited for you to thread the right color if it might put him more than 30 seconds behind schedule. You did the only thing you could. Besides, pink blends better with the black and white Snoopy-with-shades pattern on that tie than either green or red. And don't worry about the label flipping over and exposing your handiwork for all the world to see." She gave her mother a mischievous grin and stated sweetly, "Unless, or course, he decides to sprint across the parking lot."

"You didn't have to add that!" Beth exclaimed, pouting her lips and threateningly knitting her dark, peaked brows over her clear brown eyes, to send her daughter a glare from beneath that mock thundercloud.

Nan laughed and retorted, "Give it up, Mom! Just because that look could make Linda cringe, doesn't mean it will ever work on me."

Both of them smiled at the mention of Nan's older sister, who was as much like their mother as Nan was like their father. Linda had her mother's pixie looks, with the same small, peaked eyebrows, dainty ski-jump nose, and full lower lip. However, her eyes were hazel instead of brown. Like her mother, Linda usually managed to tread softly, produce a calming influence on others, and make wise choices. That's why Linda had found a good match in shy Ken Carter, whom she married two years ago. That meant moving with him to New Jersey, where he was the vital force in keeping a software company on the cutting edge of the medical billing industry.

Nan recalled her first impression when Linda brought Ken home from college one weekend. His appearance was, well, better than okay; but he couldn't seem to muster more than a dozen spoken words an hour. Nan, who was then the world's wisest ten-year-old, was sure her sister would find someone a whole lot more interesting than this guy. Wrong!

Now she wondered how she ever could have doubted Linda's impeccable judgment and could not even imagine steadfast Ken, with his ready humor, being anything other than a part of their family.

As Nan headed toward her bedroom to get dressed, she heard the phone ring, then her mother as she answered and said, "No, Fletch, you just missed him. He should be there shortly. See ya."

Chapter 3

PHIL DIDN'T MAKE it home by sunset. He missed dinner, too.

Beth called the office about 8:15, heard his voice message, and just left a terse, "I love you. Give me a call when you get a chance." She was hoping that his not answering would mean he was on his way home and that she'd be hearing the garage door respond to his remote opener within the next twenty minutes. Still she was somewhat irked that he hadn't taken the time to call when he realized he was going to have to miss dinner. How many precious seconds would that have taken? She frowned.

Beth picked up a couple of magazines from a low table and crossed the living room to ease back in a swivel rocker, her favorite armchair. It was not large enough to comfortably accommodate Phil's lanky frame. However, it was just right for her, because it allowed even the heels of her feet to touch the floor; and she loved its bright yellow floral pattern.

The contents of the room, wallpapered in vertical white satiny stripes on white, complimented the yellow and forest green of her chair and its matching floral sofa. Even the dark wooden accessory tables stood on deep green legs.

By 9:10, Beth was becoming uneasy and had quite

flipping through magazines. Nan had given up on her homework and came out of her bedroom, explaining that she couldn't even concentrate enough to read her literature assignment for Junior English. Instead, she plopped down at the piano in the living room, near her mother, and began to plunk the keys aimlessly.

Suddenly the phone rang. Beth moved quickly across the room to a lamp table beside the sofa and snatched up the green phone, anxious to hear Phil's voice as he explained what was going on. Instead, she heard a deep voice of authority say, "May I speak to Mrs. Phillip T. Vincent?"

"Speaking," she replied, her knees slowly turning to jelly. She sank onto the arm of the sofa as the voice continued. "This is Capt. Ernest Johnson, with the city police force, ma'am. I'm speaking to you from my cruiser in front of your house. May I come inside to talk to you?"

"Is it about my husband?"

"Yes, ma'am. I need to come inside and explain what has happened. I'll be right there."

"Is he all right?" she gasped as she heard the receiver click.

"Mom?" Beth could hear in Nan's voice and see in her daughter's eyes the terror she felt engulfing her own heart. The doorbell rang three times, urgently. Nan's eyes grew wider. Drawing a shallow breath, Beth murmured, "A policeman is here about your father," and rose unsteadily to her feet.

Nan bounded to the door and flung it open. The uniformed captain removed his hat as he entered the hallway, bringing with him a swirl of the night's damp chill. "Mrs. Vincent?" he intoned, glancing past the girl and into the spacious living room. Beth managed to nod, her face drained of color. "I'm sorry to inform you that you husband has been involved in a serious mishap out on Old Bonhomme Road."

ThreadBare

Nan backed across the room to her mother, and the two of them clung to each other and stared at the officer as he closed the door and stepped in from the hallway. "But is he all right?" Beth whispered.

Capt. Johnson cleared his throat twice, while he studied his shoes and wished desperately that he were not standing in this room having to say this. "Actually, ma'am," he raised his eyes to Beth's. "Mr. Vincent is dead. He apparently was killed by a hit and run driver."

Nan blurted," But wasn't he wearing his seatbelt? He always wore it! So how could he be hurt that bad with his seatbelt on?" Her blue eyes burned with denial and demanded an explanation. The officer took her mother's limp elbow and led her trancelike to the center of the sofa, where she drooped down and covered her face with her hands.

Sitting down beside Beth, the policeman looked up at the defiant girl and tried to explain. "It's a strange situation. He wasn't in a vehicle. He was on foot and must have started across the roadway."

"Are you sure he's dead?" Nan accused. "How do you even know if he's really my father?"

"He was pronounced dead at the scene by the county coroner. His body was transported to Bel-Air General at 8:20." After glancing sidelong at Beth's stricken face, Capt. Johnson continued, his voice flat and low. "All personal effects were with him, including his wallet, credit cards, checkbook, his reading glasses, his watch ... and his wedding ring."

Wave upon wave of chilling numbness swept softly through the room in the long silence that followed. Finally, Capt. Johnson turned to Beth and began again. "We need to have a positive identification of the body as soon as possible. Is there someone else who can do that for you?"

Lea Ann W. Hall

As Nan rushed over and fell on her knees before her mother, Beth swallowed hard and reached out to clasp both of Nan's hands tightly to her lap. The flat, low voice seemed to be fading in and out. "Is there a close friend, another attorney, or a family doctor?"

Squaring her shoulders, Beth said, "I think I should do this myself," and rose to her full stature.

"No, Mom," Nan entreated, jumping up. "Let Fletch do it. I don't want you to go." She turned on the policeman, who had also risen to his feet. "Why can't you just identify him from his driver's license or his law firm ID card?"

Capt. Johnson looked at the tall, slender girl standing defensively beside her mother. "And your name?" he asked gently. She told him.

"Nan, when your father was run down, he sustained massive trauma not only to his legs but also to his neck... and jaw."

Beth sagged against her daughter and collapsed before Nan could even react.

While the officer was reviving Beth with gentle pats on her face, he asked Nan if Fletch was a relative.

"He almost is. He's like an uncle to me. He and Dad are in the same law firm. I just hope he hasn't gone out of town. We sure need him now."

Chapter 4

AS IT TURNED out, Fletch Stevens did identify Phil's body. It was almost remarkable that the police were able to reach Fletch at home. He was often traveling on behalf of the law firm, a role he willingly accepted after his marriage had dissolved three years ago.

Fletch was Phil's best friend. Actually, that was because he was Beth's best friend. They had grown up together in Kirkwood and were pals during Beth's tomboy days. In high school, Fletch had decided to pursue law, and she had applauded his ambition. However, she had also begun dating, and although he mustered enough courage to ask her to the Christmas Formal their senior year, in the end the well-rehearsed words had failed him, and he had only blurted, "Do you have a date to the dance yet?"

"Not yet," she smiled, rolling her deep blue eyes at him. "But I have a pretty good idea who plans to ask me."

"You do?"

"Now Fletch, don't tell me Dick Stafford put you up to this. I've already been told that he's going to ask me to the dance. But I'm warning him. He's going to have to do the asking himself. Besides, if I work it right, I'm hoping Larry

Tobias will ask me. He wants me to sit with him at lunch today.

"That's nice." Fletch forced the pleasant words up through his dashed hopes, casting himself back into the role of pal, and even confidant. And that is where he had stayed ever since.

Fletch became a serious student of the law and worked harder at achieving success than enjoying it. Then he'd met Phil Vincent, who easily seemed to live the formula Fletch was seeking so hard to create. Fletch tried earnestly to model himself after Phil, who was a campus leader in law school while Fletch was an undergrad.

When Beth and Phil began to date, Fletch found himself getting much closer to Phil and following his lead became quite simple. It had been a good situation for Fletch. He'd picked up many points about wardrobe and decorum, as well as the legal arena itself. And best of all, when Fletch passed the bar, Phil went to bat for him, and soon they were colleagues in a great law firm.

Nowadays, the two shared a lot of running and golf time. Phil's lanky build and Fletch's wiry, five-seven frame were as familiar as a landmark to fellow golfers and dwellers along some of their running trails.

Chapter 5

"GUESS WHAT, MOM!" Nan had burst into the house, her blue eyes dancing with excitement. "Have I had an interesting day," she said over her shoulder as she bounded down the hall to her bedroom, flung her book bag on the bed, and started shedding her bright blue ski jacket.

Beth knew she'd be back in ten seconds, ready to explode with the news of what had happened at school this last Monday in January. January had been another long month of sadness for the Vincent family. This afternoon, however, Nan seemed cheerful, to say the least.

Nan's enthusiasm warmed Beth's heart, even though she had a mother's way of knowing that this wasn't going to be about some new and marvelous discovery of scholarly learning.

It had been almost three months since Phil's death. Everyone in the family had been so devastated. The holidays had plodded by as rote rituals, except for the precious time it afforded all of them to be together.

And of course, Fletch had hovered over them tenderly and guided Nan through the paperwork that continued to surface week in and week out.

As if things weren't bad enough, the family also felt achingly helpless because of the lack of answers. The unsolved case was listed simply as a hit-and-run accident. There were no significant clues. No witnesses. No enemies. No motives. No suspects. No explanations. No sense to any of it.

There were no reasons. What was Phil doing out on that desolate, remote road? Why was Phil's black Camaro found torched near a rock quarry on the Illinois side? Who had driven the car across the Mississippi, and over which bridge? Had Phil been forced from his car by some armed thug who took it? If so, did that person (or persons) purposely run him down? Why couldn't he have dived for the ditch to avoid being killed? Was he hit by another car, or was he run down by someone driving his Camaro? Is that why it had been burned to cinders?

Because no logical explanations could be found, Beth learned that the police were dissecting the case slowly and methodically, questioning numerous people who had some professional or personal link to Phil Vincent. Through close connections Fletch had created while providing legal services to Kirkwood's police department, he was uniquely able to keep apprised of the interviews of Phil's clients and casual acquaintances.

More than once as Fletch conveyed these bits of information, he'd managed to coax a smile from Beth, especially when he described how uncomfortable one of Phil's legal partners had reacted when questioned about his relationship with Phil and his whereabouts on the night Phil died. He had a solid alibi, and was not under direct suspicion, but just the idea that this supremely confident man of such eloquence when applying pressure to witnesses on the stand might be quaking in his boots was amusing to Beth.

ThreadBare

Equally funny was the picture Beth saw in her mind's eye of a banty rooster wearing tiny red cowboy boots. Perhaps this man's barely disguised envy of Phil had left him with his own sense of puzzling guilt.

Beth even chuckled about Fletch's account of the indignant retorts made by Mildred Herman, who lived across the street. Mildred resented the implication that anything untoward was going on in the Vincent household. She made it very clear that the officer should spend his time elsewhere, rather than prying into the Vincents' family life. It sounded as if she had swept the officer away just as efficiently as she swept her porch, sidewalks, and the entire street in front of her house every morning that it wasn't raining or snowing.

Then Beth's face had turned serious, as she stared at Fletch and said, "Did the police approach Mildred because they considered me to be a suspect?"

"We all are," was his gentle reply.

"Mom?" Nan said quietly, understanding her mother's expression, full of puzzled pain. Time and time again her own school friends had snapped her back from that same bewildering mind game.

Beth glanced up. "Oh, you're back. Are you ready to broadcast your bulletin to the world?"

"Yes! Yes! Yes! First, the good news. Jim Thomas asked me to the Valentine's dance, and after a two-second deliberation I decided to accept. He met me before I could even get out of Jenny's car in the parking lot! Later he explained that he knows who I carpool with because he's been casing the parking lot for two weeks. Can you believe that? He said he didn't want to take the chance of waiting at my locker and having someone else ask me before I showed up there. If you ask me, he just had the jitters. Why would he case the parking lot for two weeks, but then he couldn't wait five minutes until I got to my locker?"

"So you're pleased about this, I take it?"

"Are you kidding? I've been wanting to go out with him ever since his family moved here last fall. You know it's such a relief to have that out of the way and not have to be worrying if somebody I'd really like to go with is going to ask me. Now I can concentrate on helping Jenny and Marie and my other friends to get their dates for the dance."

"Do you mean Marie Garland or Marie Dennison?" Beth asked, trying to keep everything straight.

"Both of them" Nan laughed. "But especially Marie Garland. We've really become close since we carpool this year." Launching again, Nan pointed out, "I can also give pointers to some of the boys on how to ask a girl to the dance, without them thinking I'm begging them to ask ME." She rubbed her palms together with glee. "Playing Cupid is going to be fun!"

Chapter 6

ANOTHER LONG MONTH had passed, even if it was the shortest month of the year and, according to Nan, the Valentine dance had been a total blast. Beth had translated that to mean a success and refrained from asking prying questions.

Beth was visiting in the spacious kitchen of a good friend, Trish Cardell, where they were drinking hazelnut coffee. Jack Cardell, her husband, worked 60-plus hours a week in a successful effort to keep a chain of family-owned pizza parlors atop an economic crest, like a dauntless surfer defying engulfment by a towering wave of pending calamity.

The Cardells had two children. Their daughter, Laurie, was a couple of years older than Nan and attended Northwestern University. Brett, their son, was an adorable ten-year-old, who'd played every peewee sport available within a radius of five counties.

There had been another son, Sean, who'd died eight years ago in a sledding incident, at the age of seven, when he hit a tree head-on. Laurie, who was 12 at the time, had been on the sled with Sean. She'd suffered a broken collarbone and left arm, as well as a bad compound fracture of her left leg.

"I wish Brett was as old as his sister," Nan had lamented to her mother more than once. "He's such a doll and so much fun to be around. He's really witty for a kid his age and loves plays on words, like puns and such. I'd be willing to baby-sit him for free. But don't tell his parents that!"

Although they were 10 years apart in age, Brett and his sister had the same kind of hair. It was wavy blond and seemed to shimmer in every spot where light touched it. Hair salons make handsome profits from trying to reproduce such a stunning effect. Laurie wore hers almost as short as Brett's, with just a few soft locks framing her face and slender neck. The striking difference in the facial features of the sister and brother was in their eyes. Laurie's were like two milk chocolate drops under thick, but light arched brows. From under sandy, slanting brows, Brett's eyes seemed to reflect the blue sky of a crisp autumn day. A day perfect for football.

That's how the Vincents had first met the Cardells. Phil had been the assistant coach on Brett's football team. In the bleachers for the first home game of the season, Beth and Nan noticed Trish, who was cheering as lustily as they were.

She wore her dark hair long and clasped tightly at the nape of her neck, the rest cascading across her shoulders in loose waves halfway to her waist. Nan didn't understand how she could have waves at the ends of her hair without any sign of waves where her hair was pulled back smoothly from her face. Perhaps she used a curling iron, but Nan doubted it. Trish had a clear forehead, crowned with a small peak in her hairline, giving her a heart-shaped face that framed grey-blue eyes under slender, arched dark eyebrows, a narrow nose which Nan considered to be a little bit long, and thin lips on a wide mouth, above a tapered chin. "She looks like she's always about to ask a question," Nan told her mom, referring to Trish's high eyebrows.

During the next couple of games they waved at each other in mutual recognition. Finally, at a drizzly away game, Trish spotted Beth and came over to introduce herself, asking if Beth was Coach Vincent's wife. Beth said yes, explained why Nan had to miss this game, and invited Trish to share her umbrella to watch the rest of the misty contest as it turned into a mud-wrestling event. Of course, they talked through every play, sometimes even missing their cues to let out a loud cheer or a groan. When the game ended, they felt like they had known each other for years.

As Beth set her coffee cup in its saucer, on the Cardell's round, glass-topped wooden table, Trish said, "You ought to come to Brett's games this fall. You don't realize how Brett idolized your husband both on and off the field, so you're like an aunt to him." Before Beth could respond, Trish rushed on. "Tell you what. I'll just swing by and pick you up. Bring Nan too, if her social life will allow, what with it being her senior year and all."

As both women chuckled, Beth said, "It would be too far out of the way for you to come by."

"No, it won't. Brett vanpools with guys on the team anyway. A couple of the dads have vans . . . and the time," she added ruefully. "Besides, I wouldn't have to cheer by myself, and it would give us more time to chat."

Beth objected again, "But if you have to take me home, you might not get home before Jack does." Beth recalled Jack's tired face, with light blue eyes that always managed to brim with warmth beneath thick, slanted eyebrows slightly darker than the color of his hair. It was a good thing his short, strawberry blond hair was curly, because Jack seemed to lead a rather helter-skelter existence, and any other type of hair probably would have looked unruly most of the time. Beth scolded herself; I'm beginning to think as critically as Nan.

"So, I believe my hubby can take care of himself for a few minutes. I bet he'd still be reading and processing the mail, even if he did beat me home."

"You're pretty convincing, Trish. You should have been a lawyer."

Trish laughed lightly. "Was that an insult of a compliment? Or more to the point, was that a yes or a no?"

"Okay, you won me over. Besides, I remember Phil was so enthusiastic about the team's prospects for the coming year, what with only two of their best players moving into the next age bracket. He told me, and I quote, 'That team will be some kind of fast and scrappy bunch.' Even without Phil to assist him, it should be a great year for Coach Macklin, too,"

"Wha—at?" Beth asked, noting the look of amazement Trish was giving her.

"I thought you knew. You haven't heard? Marty Macklin won't be coaching the team this year. He switched to another league right after last season ended. He announced that his construction company will still sponsor the team, but he won't be its coach."

"You mean both of the coaches will be new? Do you know who they are?"

"Well, I heard that the new head coach is Knox or Cox or something like that. He teaches at one of the elementary schools." Trish added, "But they haven't come up with an assistant to replace Phil yet." Her voice trailed off. She knew no consoling words for Beth.

Beth chatted on. "This new guy better be good, or

the parents will be screaming to get Coach Macklin back. According to Phil, not only does that man know fundamental football, he gives his young charges his full attention."

Trish breathed a quiet sigh of relief and sipped her coffee, savoring the hazelnut flavor. Beth had mentioned Phil's name without a tremor in her voice. She really was getting better. Trish couldn't imagine though how Beth managed to cope with her husband's strange death and thought to herself that its mysterious nature had to be impeding the healing process like a festering ulcer.

Chapter 7

THAT FIRST SUMMER after Phil's death, when Nan wasn't running around with friends, she babysat a lot, both daytime and evenings—at neighbors, at the Macklins, and a few times with Brett at the Cardells. Beth realized sadly that this was just a preview of what it was going to be like around the house when Nan left for college. Maybe it was time for dear ole mom to stave off the "empty nest" syndrome by starting to give some serious thought to getting involved in some type of volunteer work, making a real commitment. Every morning before she got out of bed, Beth still asked the Almighty for the strength to make it through another day without Phil. Volunteering would probably make the effort a little less daunting.

At least when autumn rolled around, Beth had followed through and gone to a couple of the football games with Trish Cardell to see Brett play. The one this afternoon had been against Marty Macklin's team, which Brett's team had beaten soundly. It seemed strange that he'd left a team with such a promising season ahead. It was almost like he had deserted them.

She and Trish had stood by the tall, chain-link fence and spoken through it to Coach Macklin briefly before the game. He'd asked about Beth's family, with a note of genuine concern in his voice. He was not nearly as tall as Phil had been but probably weighed as much. Although his sun-streaked sandy hair was thinning some, he was still handsome in a rugged way, with a strong chin, firm lips, nice teeth, a straight nose, and hazel green eyes that gleamed from the crinkles of his tanned face. Beth also noted that he was still a sloppy dresser, totally unlike Phil. His shoes were badly scuffed, even though he could well afford new ones, the way his construction business was flourishing. The collar of his red windbreaker was doubled under against one side of his neck, too. Only the fence had curbed Beth's impulse to reach out and fix the collar for him.

Oh, she must remember to tell Nan about the Snoopy tie that Coach Macklin was wearing. It looked so much like Phil's tie, that she'd asked Trish if she recalled both coaches having one last year and whether or not they'd worn them for games as some sort of morale booster for the team. Trish said she remembered having seen the tie before, because it was such a unique design. But she didn't recall when or where or who might have been wearing it. She for sure did not remember the two coaches ever wearing matching ties together.

Later, during dinner, Beth told her daughter about the tie and asked if she'd ever seen both coaches wearing the Snoopy design tie at a game. Nan shrugged and shook her head. "No, but I'm babysitting for the Macklins next week. I'll try to remember to ask about it."

It's no big deal, dear. I just know you're so observant and in- the-know about everything that I've grown to rely on your vast wealth of knowledge."

"I get it, Mom. That's just your sweet way of saying that

ThreadBare

I'm a busybody, know-it-all that's going to get myself out on a limb someday."

"Umhmm," Beth beamed at her daughter. "You'll do just fine, if you can remember to leave the saw in the garage whenever you're climbing."

"You're pretty cool, Mom."

About a week later when Nan babysat for the Macklins, Mrs. Macklin came by in her gold Mustang convertible to pick her up. Nan was delighted that it was a mild enough evening for the top to be down. Although she'd suggested that Nan just call her Joyce, Nan felt more comfortable letting her remain as Mrs. Macklin. Always nice to Nan, she was sweet and kind. She must have been beautiful in her prime, but was a bit plump now, after having two babies, and the sharpness of her facial features seemed to have melted a little. Her turned-under blonde hair was parted low on one side, causing the other side to almost drape across one of her twinkling blue eyes. The look gave her a hint of elegance that Nan felt she herself would never be able to achieve. They rode through the lanes of suburban homes, where the windows were brightly lit and soft light glowed from the gas lampposts standing near the sidewalks leading to many of the front doors. Nan was enjoying the cool breeze that rippled through her hair.

The Macklin tots were easily entertained and begged to end the evening with a Charlie Brown video. As they trudged off to brush their teeth, still chattering about the cartoon they'd seen for the umpteenth time, and their favorite character Snoopy, Marty Junior stopped to gaze at Nan and announced, "My dad even has a Snoopy tie. There are a lot of them in the store, but the one my dad has is the best."

Nan laughed and said, "I know what you mean. My dad had a great one, too."

Nan recalled it looked like it was just a large black-on-white pattern with lots of curves in it. Then you'd take another look and realize it was made up of Snoopy faces all adjoining each other and all staring back at you. And as if that wasn't enough, the faces were each framed in those long black ears, with a set of black shades perched above a round black nose. She always thought that tie was the 'coolest.'

Sadness crept across her face as she remembered her dad that last November morning in their kitchen. He'd been wearing that Snoopy tie, too. She wondered if her mom knew where that tie was now. She made a mental note to ask her, because she hoped her mom would let her have it as a keepsake.

After both of the Macklin preschoolers were tucked into bed, Nan settled herself on the family room divan, to read her English literature assignment, but found her attention wandering. She critically analyzed her baggy lavender sweatshirt and burgundy Dockers. Maybe lavender wasn't such a good color with her auburn hair. She forced her attention back to her book and found her place in the heavy anthology again.

When she finished the reading assignment, she got up and went to check on the children. Then, as she pulled their door part way shut, she happened to glance across the hallway to the master bedroom. She wondered if Coach Macklin's Snoopy tie looked anything like her dad's.

Hesitantly, she entered the Macklin's bedroom, switching on the lights in the ceiling fan. Slowly, she crossed to the twin closets. The first one, with its door closed, was likely Mrs. Macklin's. The second one, door ajar, definitely belonged to

Mr. Macklin. It was untidy, with his shoes scattered randomly across the floor. Then she noticed a tie rack full of loosely knotted ties that was bolted to the inside of the door.

She drew nearer to the door. Without giving it a thought, she very quickly was able to spot the Snoopys in sunglasses, peering at her from around a blue striped tie. She pulled the Snoopy tie out far enough to cast full light on it. Yep, this one was exactly like the one her dad used to wear, only this one was in a loose knot, whereas her dad's always hung flat and at half-length over his racks. He'd had two racks, both compactly filled. All of his ties were the same fine brand, too, except a few that he had received as gifts.

It was rather amazing that the Snoopy tie was ever produced under her father's favorite brand name, a little far out for their usually conservative style. It must have been its subtle humor that had earned its acceptance by a company with such a prestigious image, she mused. Maybe that's what she liked so much about the tie. It was kind of like her, at least the humor part – understated but definitely wacky.

Nan was mildly surprised to find no variation of the Snoopy theme between this tie and her dad's. Perhaps the two coaches had bought them to wear as victory ties. She recalled that her father often wore his on game days. Maybe Coach Macklin did, too. As her hand continued to linger on the tie, she gently rubbed the silky texture between her thumb and fingers, thinking of her dad. Then she found herself turning the tie over lovingly in her hand. Of course, there was the familiar prestigious label. But wait! One side of the label was coarsely sewn with pink thread. How could that be? Like a hot baked potato, she let the tie drop back where she'd spied it and fled from the room, with barely enough presence of mind to turn off the fan light.

Bewilderment left her stunned. After an hour or so,

the shock wore off, crowded out by the questions that kept popping off in her mind. Needless to say, she never got any more homework finished that night. Nan just waited tensely to get home and discuss this craziness with her mother, to see what sense she could make of it. She knew Mom would be waiting up for her. When Mrs. Macklin drove her home in Coach Macklin's Lincoln, Nan was unusually quiet.

Chapter 8

AFTER NAN RELATED to her mother exactly what she had discovered in Coach Macklin's closet, her mother had remarked what an unusual coincidence that was and said Phil must have given Marty the tie sometime or other as a bond of friendship and good luck for the games. Then she came down hard on Nan for snooping through someone else's things, saying she was far too grown up to be exhibiting such inappropriate behavior.

Hot tears sprang from Nan's eyes and stung her cheeks. "Wait, Mom. I agree that I behaved badly, and you can ground me if you must. But think about this. Dad was wearing that tie the morning he left the kitchen and never came back!"

Her mother caught her breath, turning but still not quite comprehending. "Are you sure?" she asked, her cola brown eyes large in her face.

"Yes! Yes! That day is etched in my brain forever. I'm sure that's the morning you were fretting about having to use pink thread to repair the label on Dad's Snoopy tie. Don't you remember?"

"To tell you the truth, dear. I don't remember much about that day at all. Certainly not any details."

"So then how did Coach Macklin get it? The investigation

covered everyone Dad made contact with that day. I don't recall anything about Coach Macklin."

Puzzled now, Beth knew what Nan was saying made sense. But in her usual manner, she felt people must be given the benefit of the doubt. "Perhaps Phil dropped by the community center sometime during the day and gave the tie to Marty then."

"Why? They would have seen each other at practice the next day. What was the hurry? For gosh sakes, it was just a tie."

Exasperated, Beth replied, "I don't know, but there has to be some logical explanation. Tell me now, have you rummaged through your father's things, too, and couldn't find his Snoopy tie? How can you be so certain which tie he even put on that morning? I'm not that supremely confident of **my** memory."

"Mom," Nan stammered, trying to ignore that barb and the heat that was flaring up again in her heart. "I haven't been rummaging, as you call it; but how could Dad's tie be on one of his racks when I just saw it at the Macklins?"

"Fine!" Beth's eyes flashed as she turned and strode down the hallway toward the bedrooms. "Let's go rummaging!"

Reluctantly, Nan followed. By the time she reached the master bedroom, her distraught mother had flung most of her dad's ties off the first rack and onto the king-sized bed and would soon start attacking the second rack.

Nan leaned against the doorframe in a posture of helpless despair. Lamely, she began, "I'm sorry I even mentioned the tie. I thought you would want to know."

Beth made no response, finishing off the second rack and then sorting frantically through the tangled ties on the bed. Finally, she backed away, her eyes still flashing, and

ThreadBare

told her daughter, "You find it, and then you put them all back. Do you hear me? I'm going to get ready for bed." In frustration and disgust, she marched over to the master bathroom and slammed the door shut behind her.

Nan was asking herself why her heart had so much sharp pain in it and wondered if this meant she could be prone to having a heart attack at an earlier age than the national average.

By the time her mother opened the bathroom door and came out in her white satin robe and lots of face cream, Nan had smoothed out and hung the first rack full of ties and had only about half a dozen to go on the second rack. The Snoopy tie obviously was not among them.

Beth crossed to the bed and began smoothing each tie and handing it to Nan. When they were done, she reached up, enclosed her daughter in a loving bear hug, and whispered, "I'm so sorry."

The pain in Nan's heart started to melt. Nan opened her mouth to express how much she loved and needed her mother, but as their eyes met, Beth began to giggle. She turned her daughter toward the dresser mirror and pointed, giggling all the while. Reflected back at them were their embracing figures, and smears of white face cream down one side of Nan's face and on the side of her nose and in her hair.

"You look like half a clown," Beth chuckled.

"Well, that's better than looking like a whole clown the way you do every night," Nan retorted, escaping from the room to shower, wash her hair, then blow it dry. By now it was well after midnight, and on a school night, too. Oh, well. She would gladly have taken a dozen showers, and shampooed and dried her hair a dozen times, if that had been necessary to make up with her mother.

As Nan climbed into bed and turned off her lamp, she realized that the pain in her heart was gone. It had melted totally away. Then Nan heard her mother step through her half-open bedroom door. So she propped her head up, elbow on pillow. Beth's robed figure was silhouetted softly against the dim light from the hallway.

"Nan dear, I just want you to know I've been thinking about all that you told me. And I'm going to give Capt. Johnson a call in the morning to see if he has any suggestions on how to sort this all out."

"Thanks, Mom. I love you.

"I love you too, dear. Sleep well."

"You, too, Mom."

Neither of them slept well that night.

Chapter 9

BETH WALKED GINGERLY into the lobby of the police station, dressed in a pale yellow turtleneck and a brown tweed suit with a pleated skirt. Her clutch purse and low pumps were dark chocolate brown. Capt. Johnson, in full uniform, was talking on the phone but rose and motioned her over to the padded metal chair in front of his battered, wooden desk.

She hadn't remembered anything in particular about Capt. Johnson, except his name. Now, as he finished his business on the phone, she sat down and was able to study the profile of this man.

He looked to be about six feet tall as he stood behind his desk, dressed in a no-nonsense, long-sleeved navy shirt with its official badge, and matching navy slacks, a little rumpled. His body appeared to be stocky and tough. Maybe he had served in the military. His hair was dark and cropped almost too short to part.

His facial features were sharp but surprisingly warm. The nose was a little narrow, with a straight bridge and slightly flared nostrils. His ears were on the small side and set rather flat against his head. His jaw line looked strong. But she couldn't see the color of his eyes . . . she felt herself blushing and averted her eyes in shame. What on earth was she doing?

This man was clearly at least six or eight years younger than she was. She felt most uncomfortable and found herself hoping her business with him would not take long.

He'd finished his conversation and was hanging up the phone. Then he turned his full attention toward her. She's still suffering, he thought, noting the lines of distress, which softly etched her delicate face. But it was the sadness in her clear brown eyes, set in dark hollows, that sent an ache through his chest.

"Captain, I appreciate your taking time from your busy schedule to see me today."

"No problem, ma'am," he responded, unaccustomed to such civility. Then he sank into his creaking chair and added impulsively, "You can call me Ernie."

She began quickly. "I don't recall which tie my husband was wearing ... uh, which tie he had among his personal effects. Do you keep any kind of records here that would describe that type of information?

"Yes, ma'am, we do. Because this is still an open case, all of his clothing was retained for possible evidence. You probably don't remember when I explained that all to you and had you sign the paperwork. I don't suppose you'd care to say why you're making this request?"

"I'd rather see the tie first."

"Okay, let me get the file carton, so you can look through it."

"Uh...before you go, could you just bring back the tie, and not the whole carton?"

"Of course," he replied. "Can I get you a cup of coffee or tea while you're waiting?"

She smiled. "No thanks," and demurely folded her hands in her lap and let an air of patient anticipation settle over her.

Ernie was gone for quite awhile, much longer than he had intended. When he creaked into his chair, holding a tattered manila folder, he looked puzzled. "Mrs. Vincent, there was no tie." She gazed at him blankly.

"There is no tie in the carton, and the list of personal effects does not describe or even mention a tie."

"But he was wearing a suit and tie when he left home that day. He always wore a tie when he went to work. He might loosen it sometimes, but he never took it off until he got home. He didn't want to take the chance of misplacing it somewhere or wrinkling it up in a pocket.

"Mrs. Vincent," he said softly, to bring her back to the present. "I even went so far as to search through the memos attached to this case, and one of them specifically states that the subject—." He stopped to clear his throat. "That is, your husband, was not wearing a tie at the time of the accident."

"Do you think someone might have taken his tie after he was hit?" Beth asked incredulously.

"No, the marks left on the front of his sport coat and shirt by the grit of the pavement beneath clearly show that he was not wearing a tie at the time."

Trying to push troubling pictures from her mind, Beth leaned across the desk. "What if I told you that, given what you've told me today, I think I may know who has the tie my husband was wearing the day he was killed."

"I'd be most interested," he responded, his pulse quickening. "I'd also be interested to know who told you that your husband may have been murdered."

"M-m-murdered? What do you mean? I never said anything like that!"

The captain studied the dainty woman across the desk from him. Was she capable of murder? But how could that be? She'd been sitting at home waiting for her husband's return, and the phone records showed that the only phone call made from her home that evening was to her husband's office. Maybe that was a ruse. What if she had an accomplice? A lover? Then the possibilities were endless.

What was her game now? Had she planted a tie as physical evidence, which would point suspicion toward some unsuspecting dupe, maybe even the accomplice, or her lover?

The money also flashed through the officer's mind. It was definitely a significant factor. Phil Vincent had left absolutely everything to his wife, plus his firm had provided his widow ongoing payments for accidental death, as well as his substantial pension. Furthermore, she'd received double indemnity from his $1.400,000 worth of life insurance policies. Because if anything was certain, Phil Vincent had not committed suicide.

"What you said, ma'am, was that you might know who has the tie your husband was wearing when he was killed. Always before, you used the phrase "when my husband died.' You never said the word 'killed' before."

Somewhat taken aback and shaken, Beth was surprised at how sharp this man's mind was. She tried to elaborate. "All I meant was: the day he was killed by a hit-and-run driver. People can get killed without being murdered, can't they?"

"Of course," he replied, leaning back on two chair legs while the rest of the chair creaked against his sturdy frame in protest. She looked quite bewildered just now.

Besides, where was the motive? He and his team hadn't been able to dig up a thing, not a shred. Was it possible that this woman was dissatisfied with the affluence she already enjoyed and was willing to sacrifice her husband to sate her greed? The idea seemed preposterous to Ernie, but that didn't mean it wasn't true.

Phil Vincent's connections with his legal firm and all of his accounts and clients had been thoroughly scrutinized, with the firm's full cooperation. Either it really was a freakish accident of some kind or someone was extremely clever. A bit reluctantly he told himself he'd better keep his guard up.

Chapter 10

FOR A MOMENT, Ernie studied the Vincent widow as she sat stiffly before him.

"Are you aware that your husband sustained a wound to his left temple, which was not created by the tire treads?"

She cringed then asked hoarsely, "What kind of wound? Was he shot, or stabbed?"

"No, ma'am. He was struck with the corner of an unknown object. It made a deep, triangular indentation just above his ear. It may have been a piece of furniture, because several minute wood splinters, traces of varnish, and some tiny, cottony lint was detected in that wound."

"I thought you, or maybe it was the police chief, told me the car -- its tires -- had caused his injuries. Did someone hurt him first and then run him down?" Beth was trying desperately to grasp the meaning of all this.

"Whoa, ma'am, you're getting way ahead of me here. All I can tell you is what I know. The coroner said the blow to the head was severe enough to have been the cause of death, even if he hadn't sustained the vehicular injuries. So I personally decided to start treating this case like a homicide, even though it's officially classified as a hit-and-run. There are just a lot of things that don't add up. For instance, why was he already lying crosswise and face down in the road when the tires hit him."

"You could tell that, too?" she whispered, horrified.

"The coroner could." The dull ache returned to Ernie's chest, to settle deep in his heart, and his breathing was no longer effortless.

Beth nodded that she understood what he was telling her.

Ernie continued to glance at her in what he hoped was an unbiased manner. "But nothing seems to make any sense, ma'am. Did the vehicle that hit him have a chest of drawers tied to its rear bumper that also hit him? Or maybe a truck came along from the opposite direction, and its driver didn't notice a body lying in the other lane, and as it went by, a wooden box fell off and hit your husband in the head. But no chest, box, or similar object was found within a one-mile radius of where your husband's body was found."

Ernie plunged on. "So maybe he was struck on the temple elsewhere and then thrown out on the road. No matter how outlandish or logical my speculations are, either way there is no clear pattern for this case.

"I'm sorry if I'm being too blunt, Mrs. Vincent, and I didn't mean to come across so rough while ago. But ever since I reviewed the autopsy report, I've been scrutinizing this case like a hawk. There just isn't enough to go on, no weapon, no useful evidence, no motive, no suspect. Maybe it was some type of freak accident, and we just can't piece it together." He threw up his hands and dropped the front chair legs back on the floor in disgust.

"Capt. Johnson . . . Ernie," Beth almost rose from her chair to lean across the desk and gaze intently into his face. "I appreciate all your candor, your efforts, and even your roughness. I think it is going to take all that and more to get to the bottom of this."

He hoped she wasn't putting on an Oscar-winning performance. Biting his lip, he continued. "My own theory is that the only reason he was run over was in an attempt to disguise the original wound under the weight of the tires. The driver just missed his mark by a few inches." The captain was poised on the edge of his chair by this time, in case Mrs. Vincent started to collapse like she did the first night. She didn't faint. Instead, she seemed to be trying to take it all in.

Ernie had to glance away from Beth's clear gaze and shifted uncomfortably. It was bad enough that he found her to be both likeable and attractive. No way could he allow himself to experience feelings for her beyond that, because he had no evidence to confirm that this woman was not connected in some way with her own husband's death.

"Maybe what I'm about to say will help," Beth began, thoughtfully. "The reason I came to ask about the tie was in hopes that it would clear up some things. Instead, it seems that everything is coming unraveled. I do, however, know the whereabouts of the tie my husband wore that day."

She proceeded to relate to him about how Coach Macklin and Phil had coached together for eight years, and how strong their friendship had been. She wanted to omit the part about how Nancy had found the tie in the Macklin house and discovered its mended label, but realized that doing so would create more unanswered questions and mistrust. And right now she really felt the need to convince this attentive officer to believe in her.

As she finished explaining, she suddenly noticed that his eyes had flickered momentarily over her face. His dark, dark eyes. They were such a deep brown that she couldn't distinguish the irises from the pupils. She was glad to have reached the end of her story before making such a stunning discovery.

Ernie had listened intently, jotting some notes, and discreetly observing her gestures, voice inflection, and facial expressions for any telltale sign.

She plunged on. "I have a strong feeling that we can talk to Marty and find out how and when Phil gave him the tie that fateful day. Then perhaps we can build some significant leads in the case."

She sounded too articulate and smoothly professional.

"You know this Macklin guy on a first-name basis, do you?"

"Not really." As the full implication of Ernie's question dawned on her, she grew indignant. "Captain, Coach Macklin was my husband's friend, not mine. Phil . . . I was on a first-name basis with my husband, if that's permitted." Her cola-clear eyes flashed fiercely at him before she continued. "Phil enjoyed talking to me about the youngsters on their football team. He was proud of how they were growing up, living up to their potential, and developing character. He often mentioned the head coach by his first name, Marty. I always call him Coach Macklin. I guess I was so eager to hope that he could give us some kind of lead to go on that I subconsciously said his first name. I hardly know the man."

She was good...maybe too good.

"You say Nan baby-sits for them. Often? Beth didn't like the tone of the officer's voice and decided she'd had enough for one day.

"Which one drives her home, the coach or his wife?"

She rose abruptly. "His wife does." If other people had not been going about their business in this large room, she knew she would have been telling this policeman off in no uncertain terms by now. She could hear Nan's voice in the

ThreadBare

back of her head, saying, "Now, now, Mom, chill out. The man's only trying to do his job."

She took a deep breath. "If you like, Nan can get the tie the next time she baby-sits for the Macklins. Or do you want to handle this yourself?"

"Do not make any contact with the Macklins during the next 24 hours. This includes your daughter, as well as you." Beth was speechless. The officer stood and slowly stretched his arms, tightly bent at the elbows, with clenched fists, then pushed toward the ceiling, with his blunt fingers spread wide. His watch gleamed, exposed at the cuff of his left wrist. Then he relaxed, arms dropping to his sides. "We'll be issuing a search warrant."

"A what? These people aren't criminals. I'm sure they'll be glad to cooperate in any way they can." Beth was appalled at the man's casual callousness.

"Make sure that Nan does not go to the Macklin home until you hear from me, and if they try to contact either one of you by phone, tell them something's come up and you'll have to call them back in a day or two. Is that understood?" His dark eyes seemed to be trying to penetrate her protective shell.

Beth drew herself up. "I may not know the Macklins well, but I do know that they are decent, law-abiding citizens. Moreover, Nan can spot any kind of a phony a mile away." With that, she turned on her heel and started to leave.

"Mrs. Vincent, do you realize that if you or your daughter bring that tie to us, we'll have no evidence that Coach Macklin ever had the tie in his possession? It will just be your word against his."

She stared over her shoulder at the officer for a moment, like a deer caught in headlights. Then she headed straight toward the main entrance, disappearing quickly through the tall, steel double doors.

"I'll be in touch, Mrs. Vincent," Ernie said to her fading footsteps. Then he heaved a deep sign and sat down wearily. After a few moments of indulgence, he shook himself out of it. He'd always rather deal with a man than a woman, especially a recent widow.

Unconsciously he rubbed his chest with the broad palm of his left hand to ease the lingering pain, while his mind began to sort through the steps necessary to obtain a search warrant for the Macklin property.

Should he also obtain one for the Vincent property? No, that could wait for now, until he found out what he might discover at the Macklins.

Chapter 11

RATHER LATE THE following evening, Capt. Johnson called Mrs. Vincent to inform her that the tie had been recovered. He asked if he might drop by with it, to have her confirm its identify and the pink stitching as being her own.

Nan greeted him at the door, let him in, and fetched her mother. Beth confirmed that the tie was Phil's, confessing that her handiwork was far from neat because Phil had been in a hurry at the time, and then she never got the chance to redo it in white or black thread.

"That sounds like my ex-wife," Ernie remarked. "She always wanted everything to be perfect." He added ruefully, "Including me." Then he laughed hollowly, embarrassed at having said so much.

Returning to the subject at hand, he asked if Beth still had any of the pink thread she'd used on the tie. Mildly surprised, she retrieved the spool of thread for him, along with the needle, still threaded with a pink double strand about four inches long without a knot at the end. She secured the needle by jabbing it through a portion of the spooled thread and handed it to the officer. He put it all in a small, tan envelope, which he slipped inside his partially zipped, waist-fitting, navy blue uniform jacket. He tucked the packet into his shirt pocket.

"Am I interrupting something, Mrs. Vincent, or can you spare a few more minutes?"

"I always have time for anything bearing on Phil's case. Would you like a cup of coffee?" she asked, leading the way to their spacious kitchen. "It's decaf. I always make decaf the last pot of the day, and usually end up nowadays pouring half of it down the drain. Nan hasn't acquired a taste for coffee yet, so I'm not encouraging her to take up the habit."

Nan popped in as her mother was setting a couple of steaming mugs on opposite sides of the round breakfast table. "Would it be all right if I sit in on this, too, since it's about Dad?"

Beth glanced at Ernie. He nodded his okay.

"Great," Nan said. " If you want to take your jacket off, just hang it on the back of a chair. I'm going to have hot chocolate. Would you prefer that to coffee, Capt. Johnson?"

He smiled broadly at this lively teenager and said the coffee was fine. He did unzip his jacket but didn't remove it. Then he sat down and began, addressing Beth, who sat directly across from him. "I'm not sure just how much you've told Nan about –"

"Everything," she interrupted matter-of-factly. "So proceed, please."

"This afternoon, two of my men kept watch on the Macklin house until the coach arrived home from work and entered the house. Then my officers summoned me. When I got there, we served the search warrant and recovered the tie without incident."

"It took three policemen to pick up a tie?" Nan asked skeptically as she brought her mug of hot chocolate to the table and pulled a chair close to near where her mom was sitting.

Ernie chuckled, unoffended. He wagged his blunt index finger at her and said, "Wait till you hear the rest of the story." Then his demeanor became serious again.

"I asked the coach how he happened to come by Phil Vincent's tie. He managed to recall that Phil had indeed given it to him but that it had slipped his mind because he'd never actually worn it. He explained that Phil had impulsively given it to him as a good luck charm for their football team. But he couldn't recall just when or where this generous gesture had taken place.

Mother and daughter were hanging on the officer's words, transfixed.

"We decided it was time to take him down to the station to make a statement. There, under intense questioning, Coach Macklin finally was able to recover his memory. He said that Phil had given him the tie in the locker room at the community center, and he thought it happened while the team was dressing out to play their toughest opponent of last season, on a Friday late in October.

"Then one of the other interrogating officers asked if the two coaches had exchanged ties, and if so, did he think the Vincents still had the tie he'd given Phil. Coach Macklin was very cautious in answering but said he had not exchanged the tie he was wearing for the Snoopy one and that because it was so close to game time, instead of putting on the Snoopy tie, he had just hung it in his locker and had taken it home after the victory.

"Now doesn't that seem like an awful lot of detail for a guy to remember from a formerly blank memory?"

The two mesmerized listeners nodded in agreement.

"Finally, we dropped the bomb and told him that the

Vincent family would swear Phil was wearing his Snoopy tie on the day he died. Coach Macklin shrugged it off, explaining that what with the emotional ordeal the Vincent family was under, they had to be confused and that they couldn't be right, because the tie was already hanging in his own closet and had been there for several weeks."

"He's lying!" Nan blurted.

"But why would he be lying, Nan? That's what we have to figure out." Giving Beth a fleeting glance, he continued. "Where's the motive? Can either of you think of any reason why Coach Macklin would want to harm your father, or assist someone else who wanted him killed?"

After the officer left, Nan told her mom. "I like him. He's sensible; he's fair; and when he smiles his eyes twinkle. I think he's cute." Seeing her mother's deep frown, she added, "For a cop."

Chapter 12

IN THE WEEKS that followed, the Macklins did not call on Nan to baby-sit, and she was glad. She and her mother had already decided that Nan would refuse anyway. It just would be too awkward.

Meanwhile, Ernie mulled the case over and over in his mind during off-duty hours, especially as he lay in bed unable to get to sleep. It was almost a year since Phil Vincent had died. The trail was soon going to be stone cold.

A new assistant football coach finally had been named to replace Coach Vincent. In the locker room at the community center, the new coaches were supervising their young troops as they suited up for their first November game. Glen Knox, the new head coach, grew curious as he overheard some of the kids teasing Brett Cardell.

"How come you never hand out candy bars and give us money for the soda machines this season, Cardell?"

"Yeah, Cardell, don't you know we still need that energy boost after a game?"

"What, did you dad lose his job or something?"

"Nope, guys. I'm just broke this year," Brett said, shrugging it off. The others rolled their eyes.

After the game, Coach Cox heard one of the other players step close to Brett for a moment and say, "You should at least shell out to celebrate a win as big as today's was. After all, it's not every year we make the play-offs this early."

As Brett turned away from the teammate who was bugging him, Coach Knox called him over and asked him what all the ribbing was about.

"Oh," replied Brett. "I used to buy the guys stuff to eat last year. I'd bring boxes of candy bars and give out money for the soda machines."

"How could you afford to do all that last year and not now? Did I hear you say you're broke?"

Stammering a little, Brett explained. "I used to help Coach Macklin take care of the equipment last year."

"Oh, really? And he paid you? That sounds like a super deal to me."

Brett nodded, looking away and shifting his weight back and forth from one foot to the other. The nervous motion made his pale, wavy hair shimmer with highlights.

"If you want to, I'd be glad to have you help out again this year, like Scott and Joe do. But you wouldn't get paid any money. It would be strictly because you enjoy doing it."

Brett eyed the new coach warily and backed up a couple of steps. "I think I'll pass," he said, trying to appear nonchalant as he suppressed a note of distress that almost betrayed his voice.

"All right, son, you can go now." Coach Knox reached out and ruffled the kid's tousled hair. As the boy turned and dashed off to grab his gym bag, Coach Knox blinked. He knew he hadn't imagined it when Brett flinched under his touch. Ideas were beginning to bounce off each other in the mind of this young coach. And some of those ideas were starting to click together in a troubling way.

As Brett headed for the door, he glanced back furtively. Coach Knox motioned to him. Brett stopped but kept his distance. The coach stepped only a little closer, not wanting the child to take flight, and quietly asked, "How much did Coach Macklin pay you?"

"Fifty dollars each time," Brett replied softly. "May I go now, sir? My ride is waiting."

"Sure, Brett." Coach Cox watched the lad put his shoulder to the door and push quickly through it, hugging the gym bag to his chest. Fifty dollars! What had been going on here?

Chapter 13

THAT SAME EVENING, Coach Knox called the Cardell residence and reached Trish. She told him Jack wasn't home yet. Glen then asked her to have Jack give him a call after he got in that night, no matter how late. When Trish inquired if there was a problem with Brett, he assured her he just wanted to run some football strategies by Jack before they became fuzzy in his mind. When Trish hung up, she recalled that Jack usually fell asleep the few times he got a chance to watch some football on TV. So what would he know about strategies? Men, she thought to herself, shrugging her shoulders.

When Jack got home about 8:30, he returned Glen's call and agreed to meet him at a waffle house a couple of miles away. The only time he recalled meeting the new coach was at a pre-season team and parents get-together at the home of another player. When Trish started to question him about the call, he told her Glen wanted to go over some diagrams and hustled himself out the door to the garage. Anyway, that's what the coach had told him.

Arriving first, Glen explained to the waitress that he was waiting for someone and requested one of the empty booths. He didn't even bother to take off his black and white windbreaker.

His waitress went over by the cash register, behind him, and wished she were years younger. This customer was in top shape, and nice looking to boot. At least by her standards he was nice looking, broad at the shoulders and slim at the hips. He had medium brown hair with loose, short curls that tumbled over the top of his forehead and clung to the back of his neck. Wouldn't she love to get her fingers into those!

His face was rough-hewn, with nose and ears a bit large, but the curls softened his features. She sighed longingly and caught the manager giving her a quizzical look. So she put her hand to her mouth and stifled a yawn for his sake. She could even recall this young customer's eyes, gray-green with thick, dark lashes, the kind of eyes a woman could lose herself in. Oh, well . . . .

When Jack arrived, the waitress was elated to see that it wasn't a lady friend, even if he was older and didn't measure up to the young guy. The only edge he had, as far as she was concerned, was that in spite of looking pretty worn out, he was wearing a fine, dark leather jacket.

Glen offered to buy dinner. Jack said thanks but that he'd already grabbed some pizza at the last of his restaurant rounds. So they both ordered iced tea and sat in the booth looking across at each other.

"What's up, Coach?" Jack asked. "I don't see any play diagrams."

"You're right, Jack. I wanted to discuss something else with you."

"Okay, shoot. Is it something to do with Brett?"

"Yes. Were you aware that he used to treat the team to candy bars and sodas last year?"

"Oh, he may have treated a friend now and then. You're

not going to tell me that's not allowed in a player's diet anymore, are you?"

"No, Jack. I'm talking about the entire team—not just a couple of buddies."

"Sounds like those kids are pulling your leg, Coach. They're probably hoping you'll pick up on the suggestion and start treating them once in a while. Just tell them you're on to their little scheme and that they can take a hike."

"I wish it were that simple," Glen sighed wearily. "When I asked Brett if what the other players were saying about him buying them treats last year was true, he told me he used to earn money from Coach Macklin by helping him with the equipment. Did you know about that?"

"No, I didn't," Jack responded, sensing in his gut that he'd missed a boat somewhere, not able to understand why he felt this way. "I don't like the sounds of this. It's not like Brett to keep something to himself. He's a great kid about sharing what he's doing and thinking."

Glen went on. "It doesn't get better. When I asked Brett how much he got for helping with the equipment, he said, and I quote, "Fifty dollars each time."

Jack stared at Glen, his light blue eyes widening and bright with denial. "This can't be," he insisted, shaking his head again and again. Then slowly the flame in his eyes began to grow dull and glaze over, as shock set in.

Glen started to reach out to him, but Jack jerked his arm away. His eyes had turned to glinting slits of dangerous anger. His face was granite as he bashed his fist on the table. "If that creep came anywhere near to touching my son, there'll be hell to pay," he muttered between clenched teeth, bashing the table again.

Glen quickly paid the bill and hustled Jack outside before

he went totally out of control and took a notion to slam his fist though the plate-glass window.

The waitress was acutely disappointed at their sudden and disturbing departure. She'd not been able to get to the cash register in time, and the manager had been there to handle the bill.

Oh, how she'd been looking forward to touching the young man's hand, and he had paid the bill, too. Oh well, savor the good moments that come along. He had smiled at her when he first came in, a slightly crooked, but oh so charming smile.

Trying to calm Jack down, Glen exclaimed, "Hold your horses, Jack! I haven't gotten to the bottom of this yet. So don't jump to any conclusions until we know for sure what really was going on. But now do you see why I had to find out if you were aware of the situation and could give me a reasonable explanation as to why your son was getting that money?"

Jack wiped an unsteady hand down over his face. "What other conclusion could there be, except the obvious one?" Jack asked hollowly, as the damp and bitterly cold wind swept over his anger, forcing it deeper and leaving anguish in its wake.

"Your son can clear this up better than anyone else. Since I'm a coach, too, I think it would be better if I wasn't around when you talk to Brett about this, don't you?"

Jack nodded. "Do you think Brett stole the money? That he's lying and was stealing it somehow?" Torturing himself further, Jack stared vacantly across the small parking lot and mumbled to himself, "Or did Macklin have some sort of drug ring? Dear God!"

Glen put an arm on Jack's shoulder and walked with him to his car, explaining that he didn't think there was a drug connection, because guys don't usually drop out of a lucrative operation like that just because a season comes to an end.

"But what if Macklin's a pusher, and he was getting some of the players to sell for him? For God's sake," he cried out, burying his face in his hands. "My son is only 10 years old."

Glen opened the car door and Jack stumbled in, shut the door, turned the ignition, fumbled for the right button, and managed to get the car window open. Glen peered inside. "Are you going to be okay?"

"Yah, Brett will be asleep when I get back, so at least that will give me time to pull myself together." He looked at Glen through pain-filled eyes. "But how am I going to tell Trish about this?"

Glen watched with a heavy heart as Jack drove off without closing the car window. The dazed father didn't even feel the frosty dampness blasting against his hair and the side of his face.

Chapter 14

JACK CARDELL CALLED Coach Knox early the next evening and told him that Brett had stuck with the same story that Glen had coaxed from him the day before, but that he had added some details that Glen should know about.

Glen asked, "The waffle place again?"

"No, just come on over to the house. Trish and I both want to talk to you. We're about a mile and a half west of Cherokee, on the north side of Clayton Road. He gave Glen the house number.

"What about Brett? It could make him mighty uneasy to see me in his home."

"We decided he shouldn't go to school today, so Trish drove him over to her parents near Springfield, Illinois. That's what he wanted to do. They love Brett all to pieces, and spoil him a bit, too. But they raise cocker spaniels, and he really loves to help out. We'll go back over Friday night and bring him home Sunday afternoon. He knows he can call Trish anytime, if he gets to feeling homesick."

"I'll see you in half an hour," Glen said, digging in his pants pocket for the car keys.

Glen admired the spacious and pleasantly lit landscaped lot as he pulled up in front of the Cardell's place, noting the attached three-car garage. Before his hand could reach the doorbell, Jack pulled open the door, having seen Glen's approach from the den window. He looked haggard but acted perfectly normal as he greeted Glen.

Trish was the gracious hostess, taking and hanging his jacket in the foyer closet. However, she too, looked like she had not slept much last night. Glen looked admiringly toward the living room, taking in the lovely shadings of deep rose and powder blue. Then he realized the Cardells were heading toward the back of the house, expecting him to follow them into their great room.

Near a huge, red-brick fireplace, Trish invited Glen to sit down in one of the six oak chairs, with flat arms and comfortable spindled backs, gathered around a glassed-topped round table supported by a massive pedestal leg. The table was also oak. But it reminded Glen of his great-grandmother's old maple table.

Trish settled herself in another chair, while Jack busied himself at the kitchen island. Topped with deep green marble, the glistening counter surface looked large enough for Glen to envision a white boat, a 14-footer, floating on it with room to spare. There, Jack filled three mugs from the steaming coffee maker and carried them to the table, where he slid a mug to each of the others and sat down with his.

Jack and Trish exchanged glances, which Glen found inscrutable. Jack sipped gingerly from his steaming mug then looked at Glen over its rim. Getting directly to the point, he set the mug down and said, "Trish and I told Brett this morning, right at this table, that you had talked to me because you were concerned about him and thought there was more than met the eye about being paid by Coach Macklin to take care of football equipment last year."

"How did he react?"

"He broke down crying. He was sobbing and shaking so much that I couldn't even understand what he was saying. Trish suggested that she take him over to the divan while I turned on the fireplace logs. Then I went over and sat on the other side of him. We just kept rocking him in our arms and shushing him and reassuring him until the sobs subsided. Then finally he grew still."

"You sound like super parents," Glen said, trying to control the awe in his voice. He was well aware of how many parents would have resorted to accusatory and defensive tactics, focusing on their own sense of guilt or their anxiety about damage to their own images, instead of providing an atmosphere of unconditional love and assurance for their child.

"We didn't know what else to do," Trish said. "It was obvious he was hurting so much."

Chapter 15

JACK CONTINUED THE deep conversation around the Cardells' oak table, "Bit by bit, Brett began to tell us; and the facts just started tumbling out."

"Can you imagine this?" Trish asked, hot with indignation. "Coach Macklin asked Brett if he'd like to help out with the equipment. Of course, you know Brett. He was pleased that the coach asked him to help out and was ready to pitch right in. Well, the coach called Brett aside at the next practice, as all the other kids were heading outside to do warm-ups with Coach Vincent.

"When no one was left around, the coach motioned him into the equipment room. Brett questioned why he was supposed to work in the equipment room during practice, when most of the equipment was out on the field. The coach said something about taking care of what was still there. Then he stepped over, closed the door, and locked it. Brett asked him why he was doing –"

"Get this!" Jack blurted. "The coach told Brett that because he was such an outstanding young man, he wanted to have a little talk with him and this would all be a nice secret between the two of them. Nice, my foot! You know what happened."

Jack bowed his head as his voice faltered. Trish reached across the table to take hold of her husband's hand. He gripped hers tightly.

Lifting his head, Jack continued. "Afterwards, when he unlocked the door, Coach Macklin unfolded a crisp fifty-dollar bill from his shirt pocket, winking at Brett and ruffling his hair, and told him he'd earned it! It's a good thing Trish was here with us, or I'd have gone after Macklin right then and there."

Trish picked up again. "This went on, again and again, at different times, Brett told us." Trish swallowed hard a couple of times. "And each time Macklin cheerfully forked over a fifty-dollar bill. He also cautioned Brett not to say anything to anyone, telling him that to do so would ruin his hopes of ever playing sports for any other coach. Can you believe this guy? I can even recall one time when Coach Macklin brought Brett home late after one of the games, explaining that there must have been a mix-up and that my son had missed the van-pool ride. And to think I actually thanked that man because I thought he had done us a favor!"

"I hope you plan to press charges," Glen suggested softly. "The man's still coaching."

Jack and Trish exchanged a long glance. Then Trish looked at Glen. "We haven't even discussed that yet."

"It gets worse, Glen," Jack clipped.

"Excuse me? Worse than this?" Glen asked. Then looking incredulously from Trish to Jack. "There were others?"

"We don't know about that," Jack replied. "But listen to this. One day last season, Macklin had the gall to meet Brett as he was getting on his bike to leave school. Can you believe that?" Jack continued, looking over at Glen. "Right there in front of everybody, he put Brett's bike in the

ThreadBare

trunk of that huge Lincoln he has and drove him over to the community center, where the locker rooms are . . . to that equipment room."

Glen lowered his head and shook it in disbelief and disgust. "That fiend!" The knuckles of his clenched fists grew white.

"But get this, Brett said when it was over, Coach Macklin unlocked and opened the door, then took the fifty-dollar bill from his shirt pocket to hand to him. But this time Coach Vincent was coming around the corner."

Glen could visualize the short hall, with the equipment room located at the end of it, and its T-intersection with the main hallway, about six feet long. So the two coaches must have been squared off at each other, only a few feet apart.

"What's going on here?" Brett heard Coach Vincent demand as Macklin chuckled and said, "I thought the kid deserved a little something for scrubbing all the helmets." He crammed the bill into Brett's fist and told him to be on his way.

"Brett had to tell Macklin that he needed his bike first," Jack said. "Coach Vincent came out, Brett said, and stood on the sidewalk, watching while Macklin got the bike out of his car trunk. As soon as he could get on it, Brett skirted the Lincoln and took off as fast as he could pedal. He glanced over at Coach Vincent as he rode by and heard him yelling at Macklin about that fifty-dollar bill and Macklin still trying to laugh it off and convince Coach Vincent that it was just a five spot. The last words Brett heard were Coach Vincent's retort that Macklin still had some big-time explaining to do about locking that door from the inside."

Thoughtfully, Glen murmured, "But Coach Vincent never did anything about this. I find that hard to believe. He was such a first-class guy. I've been told he was actually the best coach in the conference, but he always chose to assist, because with his law practice he couldn't always be certain he'd be there for all of the workouts."

The room was quiet, except for a clock ticking somewhere. Jack wore a granite face except for the muscles that were working where his jaw was hinged, and tears were trickling down Trish's cheeks.

"Glen," Trish said in a whispery voice. "At this point in his story, Brett burst into tears again and told us, 'Coach Vincent was the nicest man I ever met. I was hoping he might find a way to help me. But then the next day you told me he'd died in a car accident. So then I knew my hopes were all gone.'"

"That poor kid," Glen said with a catch in his throat.

Trish pushed on. "But, Glen, Beth Vincent has told me there's a possibility that Phil was murdered. Do you think the police know that Macklin saw Phil on the day of the accident? Maybe he knew where Phil was going when he left the community center, or who he was planning to meet."

"Don't you think Macklin would have told the police about seeing Phil on that particular day?" Glen asked.

"Not if Macklin isn't aware of the possibility that Phil was murdered," Jack pointed out.

"Do you want me to confront Macklin about this? Challenge him about Brett?" Jack asked boldly.

"Oh, no!" Trish gripped the edge of the table with both hands, staring first at her husband and then at Glen. "No confrontations. We should work with the police on this. Let's just do it one step at a time."

Jack replied haltingly, like he was thinking of each solitary word as he said it. "You are right, hon. I will discuss this with Chief Kinard in the morning. Then we will regroup and figure out the best steps to take against Macklin." At this point, his voice ceased to be jerky and took on a strong note of conviction. "Whatever we decide on, our son is our number one concern. We must protect his sanity, dignity, and privacy." He rose slowly and deliberately from his chair.

"I'd rather Glen handle this first step," Trish said softly, reaching for Jack's hand.

"She's my anchor," he explained sheepishly, sinking back into the oaken chair. "I tend to lose my temper sometimes. Do you mind going to see the chief?"

"No problem," Glen said, recalling Jack's fist pounding from last night. Besides, he was glad to be making some kind of contribution to this shattered family.

Chapter 16

POLICE CHIEF DONOVAN Kinard was not tall, but he was a former marine and could probably still fit into his military uniforms. His hair, a mixture of salt and pepper, was short, in spite of the balding spot that was trying to materialize on the crown of his large head. No camouflage of longer, wispy hair for this guy. His broad face sported lively blue eyes, a rather flat nose with a scar across the wide bridge, and tight lips that occasionally split into a grin of big, sparkling teeth. His ears were set tightly against his head. He was built like a bulldog. Thick everywhere except in his bowed legs. Idly, Capt. Johnson tried to visualize what his boss would look like in a pair of walking shorts.

The chief looked over from his office doorway, where he was standing with his burly arms crossed, and saw the captain's bemused expression. He motioned for him to come into his office. Ernie responded, telling himself surely his boss couldn't read his mind.

"Did you notice the guy I was just talking to?"

"Kinda curly-headed fellow that left a minute ago?"

"Yeah, that's Glen Knox. He's a second-year P.E. teacher over at Winchester Elementary and coaches small-fry football. Took Coach Macklin's place. Must know his game pretty well to fill those shoes."

"Not only does he know his football," Ernie replied, "he's a pretty good third baseman and a fair slugger, too. He and I played on the same county softball team last summer. We kinda had a contest going between us to see who could hit the most homeruns."

"Oh, really," the chief looked at Ernie with a new glint of interest in those blue eyes. "Who hit the most and how many?"

"We wound up tied, sir. Both of us hit nine homers."

When the chief had finished relating about what the Cardells' son had told his parents, he said, "Just bring Coach Macklin in for questioning, and we'll take his statement. Maybe he can give us something to go on, tell us if Vincent said anything about where he'd be going, or if anyone called Vincent, or if he recalls any suspicious vehicle around the community center parking lots on that day, anything."

Pausing as he started out through the office door, Ernie looked back and said, "Chief, I hope this isn't another blind alley. I hope to God it isn't."

Capt. Johnson talked to Macklin's secretary in the main office of his construction company, just a few blocks down from the police station. She told him the location of the job site where her boss was.

When Ernie found Macklin, he had to wait several minutes for Macklin to extricate himself from a small bunch of workers wearing insulated work clothes, still shouting stern Spanish instructions to them on frosty breath as he broke away and approached the officer. He wore a brown plaid sport coat and matching brown slacks. Although Ernie

ThreadBare

was wearing gloves and had the collar of his heavy uniform jacket turned up, he figured Macklin to be the type who would disdain the thought of an overcoat and gloves.

"Wanta ask me about another tie, Sarge?" Macklin quipped, sparks of defiance flickering from deep in his greenish eyes.

"Nope, but Chief Kinard wants to talk to you now."

Macklin raised his eyebrows and the defiant sparks died away. "He wants me at the station?"

"Yep."

"Now?"

"'Fraid so."

Pursing his lips, Macklin looked back at the job site workers and waved, to signal that he was taking off. Under his breath, he said to Ernie, "You can call in and tell your chief I'm on my way."

"Ernie nodded curtly. " I'll be right behind you."

As Macklin drove along the country road, headed for the police station, he caught glimpses of the patrol car in his side-view mirrors. *That captain has it in for me. I could see it in his eyes*, he thought. *He thinks the Vincent women are telling the truth about Phil wearing that Snoopy tie the day he died. But it's just their word against mine.*

Glancing into the rearview mirror as they slowed for the stoplight near the police station, Macklin could only see a bright reflection off the cruiser's windshield staring back at him. He thought, *I know this cop thinks I'm a liar. Let's hope I don't see the same expression on Chief Kinard's face that I saw on that captain's while he was waiting on me out at the site. What in blue blazes does the chief want with me anyway?* Macklin felt an icy hand curling slowly around his heart, attempting to freeze his blood flow.

When the chief talked to him, Macklin played innocent

and indignant at the Cardells' accusations. It was all Ernie could do to contain himself as the chief finally dismissed Macklin and they watched him stomp out and slam the chief's office door hard enough to crack the right upper corner of its windowpane.

Chapter 17

THE NEXT WEEK, Coach Knox visited the Cardells to fill them in on a detailed account of the exchange between himself and Chief Kinard. He'd called them the day he talked with the chief, but had just given Trish a simple briefing.

After explaining how he'd told the chief what Brett had confided to his parents, Glen asked them. "That takes care of Step One. Have you two decided what the next step should be? About pressing charges?"

Trish spoke up, glancing quickly at her silent husband. "Jack agrees with me on this, although less than whole-heartedly. A good friend of my mother is a psychologist here in West (St. Louis) County. I want to take Brett there first and discuss the situation with her. I've already talked to her on the phone, and we set up an appointment for tomorrow."

"I see," Glen nodded, feeling an unseen door closing quickly in his face. From here on, he would be out of the loop.

"Since the following day is Saturday, and the kids' play-offs don't start until next week," she went on, "we'd like for you to join us for lunch, if you're not too busy. I know this Saturday will probably be hectic for a coach who hasn't had

Lea Ann W. Hall

a Saturday off since August, but we'd love for you to make it if you can. If an evening meal would be better, we could do it then instead."

"Seems like I'm over here all the time," Glen mumbled.

"Glen," Jack answered. "Trish and I owe you a lot, and this is just one way of letting you know how much we appreciate what you did and continue to do for Brett. After all, buddy, since our first meeting at the waffle place, you've become an important part of our lives."

Feeling the warmth rise in his neck, Glen said, "On one condition. I'll bring the dessert. No need for alarm. I'm pretty good in the kitchen when I put my mind to it."

As Glen stood in the foyer, accepting his jacket from Jack, Brett bounded down the steps, from his room upstairs, and looked up into Glen's face. "Hey, Coach, thanks for helping me."

Glen knelt gently beside the boy, looking into those sky blue eyes, while his parents looked on. "Is anyone bothering you now the way Coach Macklin did?" Brett shook his head emphatically. "Has he ever come by your school again?"

"Nope. I haven't seen that man since the day you became our coach. I think you must have scared him off."

At that, they all laughed. Moments later, as Glen started his car, he noted that the warmth that had begun in his neck and face had spread pleasantly clear down to his toes. He waved back at Brett, who was waving at him from the den window.

Two days later, Glen was back in the Cardells' foyer, surrendering a pan of brownies to Trish before shrugging off his coaching jacket and laying it across the seat of a small wooden chair.

"Jack's just working a half day, so he'll be home any minute," Trish said as they walked back toward the great

ThreadBare

room. "Oh, and if you hear a ruckus from down below, we let Brett invite three of his pals over. And they're going to have a picnic in the basement," she added with special emphasis and a quick wink.

"Is anyone else from the team down there?" Glen asked, as Trish set the brownies on the emerald island counter, lifted one corner of the foil top, and took a deep, appreciative sniff.

"Oh, no. These are some pals that he's been friends with ever since he started to school, a trio of hyperactivity."

Glen shook his head, chuckling. "They grow up fast, don't they?"

"I hope not too fast. They're supposed to be playing board games. But it sounds awfully quiet down there."

"Mind if I take a peek?"

"By all means, please do! And let me know if I need to scotch them for anything!"

Halfway down the carpeted, open stairway, Glen could see the four youngsters, clustered tightly around a sturdy game table. Quietly, he backed out of sight and retreated to the kitchen.

Trish raised her arched eyebrows a little suspiciously when she saw Glen approaching with his index finger intersecting his lips. "What's so hush, hush?" she queried.

He whispered, "There is a serious arm-wrestling match going on down there, and I didn't want to break Brett's intense concentration."

Glen sat down at the big round table, and a mug of steaming black coffee appeared magically at his elbow. Visiting the Cardells had certainly opened his eyes to some of the advantages of marriage, most of which were a lot more meaningful than being served coffee.

Jack came home and began chatting while he washed

up at the kitchen sink. Trish, working efficiently around him, finished bringing the food to the table.

Boisterous peals of laughter, followed by mock protests and renewed challenges, floated up the stairs. Trish explained to Jack, "They're having another one of their arm-wrestling tournaments."

Jack was smiling as he and his wife joined Glen at the table. Growing thoughtful, he looked at Glen. "Remember that lady psychologist Trish told you about? Hon, you were more than impressed with her, weren't you?

"She thinks it may be a minimum of six months before she can complete a case study to submit as evidence. That way Brett won't have to make statements directly to law enforcement or other officials, at least for a while. However, she does think Chief Kinard should be notified of the assaults immediately. Maybe he can get a confession from Macklin. But she thinks all this should be handled without Brett's knowledge at this time."

"Sounds like she's got Brett's best interests at heart," Glen said, helping himself to a barbecued pork steak."

"That's what I thought," Trish nodded, as they passed the food around.

Then they all three held hands while Jack offered up a brief prayer. Glen felt strangely like he was a soldier who'd just come back to civilized living from somewhere out in the trenches.

While they ate their meal, they discussed Step Two. Both parents agreed that it was imperative to press charges. Since it was his parents that Brett had confided in, Glen suggested they would be the logical ones to speak to Chief Kinard. They were in the best position to answer his questions and could furnish a complete statement. Jack ribbed Glen about not wanting to take on another task for them, then quickly acknowledged that Glen's suggestion made absolute sense. Trish agreed.

Footsteps padded up the basement steps. "Mom, where's our picnic?"

"You go get the old quilt out of the closet down in the game room," Trish instructed, rising from the table. "Hot dogs with mustard and relish, chips, carrots, celery stuffed with cheese, and brownies coming up! And the paper plates and napkins are here on the tray."

Brett halted in mid-stride toward the stairs. "You baked us brownies?"

"No, Coach Knox did."

"Honest?" Brett asked, shooting Glen a look of new respect. Then an impish grin spread over his face as he stared down his coach. "Wait until I tell the team that you cook! By the way, Mom, you can skip the carrots."

"You wish," came her quick retort.

Chapter 18

ON MONDAY, JACK and Trish went to see Chief Kinard with dread tugging at their hearts. They just wanted to get the ordeal over with.

Cpt. Johnson watched a well-groomed couple in their mid-thirties enter the chief's office, and wondered what was up. It was more than an hour before the chief opened his office door, and the married couple departed. That is, Ernie assumed they were husband and wife. Their countenances were gravely serious as they left, holding hands; and they appeared shaken.

The chief motioned to Ernie, "Come on in, and bring your mug and one of the coffee pots."

Ernie's pulse quickened. This might be interesting as well as lengthy, he noted with satisfaction. Shoving back his chair, he got up from his desk and stretched thoroughly in all directions. This should be good.

After fetching the coffee pot and replenishing his mug and the chief's, Ernie settled himself in the only other padded, metal chair in the room. Both had arms on them. He wished his desk chair had arms. Maybe he could make a swap with the chief, but squelched that idea as soon as it popped into his mind. He peered expectantly over at the chief, who was standing at the bulletproof window with his hands clasped behind him, surveying a broad scope of the quiet lane. On this side were a few parked cars, bordered by some young trees and a little grass. Across the street stood the first block of a neighborhood of old three-story houses, flanked with rambling porches and bulwarked with century-old trees, in yards large enough to balance the imposing structures.

"Squirrel gazing or leaf watching?" Ernie queried, impatient to be briefed.

"What am I watching?" the chief responded. "A couple of heart-broken parents getting into their car and driving away.

"Who are they, and what did they want?"

The chief did not respond for a moment and did not turn from the window.

"They are the parents of Brett Cardell, and they are thirsting for revenge against an evil man. But they are not foolish enough to allow their rage to circumvent the justice system and risk jeopardizing the future well-being of their family. You see, actually, they are very smart parents, even in their grief."

Slowly, almost woodenly, Chief Kinard came over behind his desk and slumped down in his chair. Then he nearly drained his coffee mug. Finally, his blue eyes met Ernie's dark ones, and in a low monotone, he began to tell the gut-wrenching story the Cardells had just laid before him.

First, he told Ernie that the Cardells were the owners of a string of pizza restaurants, one which most of the police force frequented at one time or another. Ernie nodded his recognition. Then the chief began to relate how the suspicions of Coach Knox had been aroused concerning the Cardells' son.

Ernie told himself he should be taking notes, but his body felt glued to the chair, and he didn't stir. That is, not until

ThreadBare

he heard Macklin's name in connection with the insidious behavior. Then Ernie jabbed his fist in the air and shouted, "YES! That man reeks! He may not be a murderer, but child molestation is going to make his time in jail seem like a life sentence."

The chief continued, "By the way, remember when we questioned Macklin and he described the day that Phil Vincent died as being, and I quote, 'just plain ordinary'? That's not the way young Brett Cardell remembers it."

Ernie whipped his notepad out of his shirt pocket and began scribbling notes as fast as the chief's words flew off his tongue. At the end, Ernie read aloud the part about where, as he fled on his bike, Brett had overheard Coach Vincent's heated conversation with Macklin.

Bolting to his feet, Ernie's dark eyes were ablaze. "Chief! This is motive. We've got motive!" The thud of Ernie's upset chair added convincing emphasis to Ernie's discovery.

"Hold on, Captain," the chief admonished. While Ernie righted his chair, the chief carefully pointed out, "You may have motive, I said may have. But never forget this. You can't go jumping to conclusions or stretching holes in speculation. Get the hard evidence. And while you're tracking this down, keep telling yourself over and over that things are never quite the way they seem."

Ernie's mind dutifully absorbed the sage advice his boss was spouting at him. Then while the end of that last sentence burned in his head, Beth Vincent's face filled his mind. Surely there couldn't be a connection between her and Macklin, could there? Heaven forbid!

"Can you get one of the other guys to tie up any loose ends you've got, so you can get on this ASAP?"

Ernie blinked to clear his head and nodded to the now pacing chief that he understood.

"Good! As soon as I find out Macklin's whereabouts from his secretary, I'm sending three cars after him. And no, YOU are not going!" He'd stopped to point a finger at Ernie. "I want you to produce the following info faster than anything you've ever done for the force."

The pacing resumed. "1. Get over to the courthouse and obtain a search warrant for the Macklin residence, including house, grounds, garage, tool sheds, chicken coops, you name it.

2. Process the paperwork to impound all vehicles, of any description, belonging to Macklin or his wife, as well as any vehicles not in working order that are found on the property.

3. Also, get search warrants for the properties of any structures Macklin has under construction."

Ernie's heart was beginning to pound with excitement and determination. The chief continued to pace, scratching his head. "4. Start the rookie going on the computer to determine if the Macklins own any other property, in or out of Missouri, and coordinate search warrants for any found in-state. I'll make the out-of-state contacts if necessary.

5. Get someone in Records to begin the procuring process for phone records, credit card statements, any accessible financial records. Got it?"

"Yes, sir!" Ernie's "shorthand" was in cruise mode.

"Oh, and 6. Contact both roaming patrol cars and have the officers here ready to start searching the job sites as soon as we have the warrants in hand!"

Taking in a deep breath, he turned toward Ernie in mid-pace and ordered, "Sgt. Logan and I will take a couple of the guys out to handle the Macklin place.

"When you've finished 1 through 6, I want YOU to expand this investigation. Determine if the creep ravaged

ThreadBare

any other kids. Tomorrow's front-page story on Macklin's arrest may help bring something out of the woodwork."

The chief had stopped his pacing and looked sternly at Capt. Johnson. "As for the Vincent case, I want you to put that investigation on a back burner until we've nailed this savage predator's hide to the wall." Between clenched teeth, he added, "Far, far away from kids."

Jaw tight and breathing heavily through his nose, Chief Donovan Kinard looked incredibly formidable. Relieved that he didn't have to reckon with this fire-breathing dragon, Ernie strode purposefully back to his desk, keeping his notepad out of his shirt pocket. He bent over his desk and made a phone call to the courthouse with his left thumb and picked up a pen with his right hand.

Moments later, Ernie heard the chief's car lunge out of the lot, its siren screaming. The chief was racing to back up the actions of his men. Ernie could hear other distant sirens converging.

Macklin's secretary must have said her boss was in his office this morning. Good! The TV vans would probably get there faster than if Macklin was out at one of the job sites. Maybe tonight's news coverage would show the "savage predator" in handcuffs.

Ernie smiled tightly and admitted to himself that Chief Kinard had a way with words when he got riled up.

Chapter 19

AFTER BEING CONFRONTED with the evidence, which Macklin was told would include not only Brett's statement but also a statement by Coach Knox and statements from football team members about Brett's generous treats the previous year, as well as statements from a couple of schoolmates who recalled seeing the football coach talking to Brett after school one day last fall and actually insisting on putting Brett's bike in the trunk of his car, Macklin confessed.

No one else came forward with similar charges of molestation against Macklin. So apparently Brett was his only current victim. Who knew what might lie in Macklin's past.

With the guilty plea, and under the new expediency court reform passed by the Missouri legislature, Macklin was quickly sentenced and took up residence in the state penitentiary for a period of at least eight years. He left his broken-hearted wife and their two youngsters in the hands of a competent financial attorney from the law firm where Phil Vincent had been a partner.

Chapter 20

ERNIE WENT FISHING for a couple of days after the Macklin case was closed. He had even foregone this year's softball season, and now he was in bad need of a break. With a couple of good buddies who weren't policemen, he went on a relaxing trip down to Tablerock Lake, in Missouri's southwest corner -- Branson territory. It seemed like the fish were just lurking beneath the surface, longing to jump into their boat. The month of May is always a good time to go fishing in America's heartland.

Now he was ready to renew his efforts to solve the Vincent case on his desk, ready to sniff out and track down the person or persons responsible for the attorney's death. Ernie wanted to start by reading the exact words Brett Cardell thought he'd heard between the two coaches as he cycled away.

First, he stretched his compactly muscled arms and shoulders thoroughly, appreciating the greater freedom the short sleeves of his light blue uniform shirt afforded. It took Ernie a while to locate what he was after, rifling through set after set of stapled pages.

Finally, he stopped in the middle of one set. Bending the top sheets back over the staple, Ernie clutched the sheath of papers in one hand and began unconsciously to run the blunt fingers of his other hand through his short-cropped hair. Here it was, the statement that Brett's psychologist had submitted on his behalf.

It read: Afterwards, when Coach Macklin went over to unlock the door (to the equipment and supply room of the south locker room in City Memorial Community Center (CMCC)), he turned the lock in the doorknob and was going to hand me the fifty-dollar bill. As he opened the door, I saw Coach Vincent, who'd just walked around the corner.

He asked what was going on. Coach Macklin just laughed and made some comment about me deserving a little something for cleaning up the football helmets. Then he shoved the bill into my hand and told me to leave. I had to remind him that my bike was still in the trunk of his car.

Coach Vincent came outside [south entrance to CMCC, leading to the west parking lot] and stood on the sidewalk, watching with a big frown while Coach Macklin got my bike out. Then I jumped on my bike and got out of there. I pedaled by Coach Macklin's car as fast as I could and sneaked a glance at Coach Vincent as I raced by. He was shouting at Coach Macklin about the fifty-dollar bill, and Coach Macklin was laughing about it being a five spot. (I knew what that meant from watching stuff on TV.)

Since I'm supposed to be telling the whole truth, after I got a couple of blocks away, I slowed down a little and coasted while I dug the crumpled bill out of my jeans pocket, thinking maybe Coach Macklin really had given me a five-dollar bill. But it was another fifty, big as life.

After my folks told me Coach Vincent had died, I waited until the next weekend, when my parents were both outside. My dad was using the leaf blower to clear leaves off the driveway, and my mom was brushing leaves off the front

ThreadBare

shrubs with a broom. She does that a lot in the fall. They thought I was finishing my homework, which I was. But when I saw that the coast was clear, I put that fifty-dollar bill right down the garbage disposal, running the water on full blast for five minutes afterwards. It didn't seem right to treat my teammates, what with Coach Vincent being dead and all. When I explained to the guys that this wasn't the time for treats, no one griped. They understood.

After listening to this stuff I put on the recorder, I realized I left out something. When Coach Vincent was arguing with Coach Macklin about the money, he said something else. It was the last thing I heard as I was hightailing it. He told Coach Macklin that he had some tall explaining to do about locking the door from the inside. At first, I thought Coach Vincent meant that he and Macklin were locked outside. But I knew that you can't lock the entrance doors from the inside. They have to be chained. So then I decided he was talking about the equipment room door and must have heard the lock pop when Coach Macklin was ready to open the door. By this time, I'd started slowing down a little and thinking about how I'd better take a close look at that bill in my pocket.

At the time, I was really scared of Coach Vincent, because it wasn't like him to get all mad. But at the same time, I felt like he was on my side, not Coach Macklin's. I really miss Coach Vincent. I'm sure glad Coach Knox came to our team though. He's mega cool. And he's the one that's helping me get Coach Macklin away from me and all kids for good.

Ernie tossed the papers onto his desk and rubbed his eyes with a thumb and forefinger. I'd better make a copy of this, he told himself. Then I'll start pouring over the whole stack, searching for any kind of clue that could explain what had happened after Brett rode away on his bike. Had anyone seen or talked to Vincent, even by phone, after that? Had there been anything found in the Macklin searches that might prove significant? What about the vehicle reports? He'd look that up first, just as soon as he grabbed some lunch. After all, Ernie was sure Phil Vincent didn't get clear out on Old Bonhomme Road on foot.

The report on Joyce Macklin's gold Mustang convertible was pretty mundane. There was one intriguing note about her husband's white Lincoln, concerning some bits of fiber tufts found on the deep blue seat cushion in the back. It appeared that they derived from white terry cloth material.

The only other item from any of the reports that caught Ernie's attention was the report on siftings from Macklin's backyard barbecue pit, described as being a brick oblong— six feet by three and a half feet at the base and 30 inches high, with a five-foot stack at one end. The only curiosities among the charred gleanings were several small objects of various metallic compositions. There was a thin piece of metal, a symmetrical oblong with the numbers 1995 etched into it, and the remnants of several delicate screws.

Ernie knew he was overdue for a visit to the Vincent home, even if he didn't have much of an update. He could have just as well made a phone call, but he felt like he could read people a lot better in person. He wanted to see Beth Vincent. He tried to reassure himself that he really did need to be able to scrutinize her facial expressions in order to conduct a truly competent investigation. No half measures here.

ThreadBare

When he visited the Vincent household, the place was aswirl with Nan's activities, a pending graduation and a summer job at a Minnesota camp for kids. Nan had led him into the living room and was gushing about all her plans when Beth came across the dining room from the kitchen in a green mint sweatshirt, faded jeans, mint green socks, old tennis shoes and no earrings. (Now why would he notice a thing like that? Must be that detective training.) She was smiling and drying her hands on a dishtowel. He was glad he'd come in person. After all, how could he describe the charred objects over the phone?

Deftly, Ernie sprinkled the metal objects from their tan envelope onto an end table near Beth's floral chair and asked for comments. Nan picked up the blackened piece of flat metal. "This looks like something that you might fasten to the collar of a large dog. Do you suppose it's some kind of a rabies tag?" she queried, then added, "But the Macklins don't even have a dog." Beth had no suggestions of her own.

When Ernie took his leave, he found himself thinking of Beth as he returned to the station. Why was his mind even calling her Beth? She was Mrs. Phillip T. Vincent, widow, and possibly an accomplice to her husband's murder. Period! He tried to persuade himself that when this case was solved, his mind would get back to normal; but his persuasive abilities weren't at all convincing. He had a strong hunch that nothing would ever be the same again.

Chapter 21

ERNIE WAS BECOMING increasingly annoyed at his lack of progress on the Vincent case. There was so little to go on. His sleep was troubled. He would get up and walk aimlessly about his apartment, then fall back into bed and close his eyes tightly, trying to will himself to sleep. Worst of all, he was getting grumpy.

Maybe he'd show up at softball practice tomorrow night and talk to Glen Knox about the case. Then he decided just to go ahead and leave him a message to call between classes or after school was over for the day.

When Glen returned the call, Ernie answered brusquely and explained that he needed to see if the two of them could sort out any new angles on the Vincent case. Glen said, "I hear you, man. Your frustration is beaming through loud and clear." After a pause, he continued," Have you ever been over to the locker rooms?"

"You mean at the community center?" Ernie asked, a bit puzzled. "I've been to the CMCC plenty of times, but never in the locker rooms."

"Since that's the place Coach Vincent was headed when he ran into Macklin and Brett, why don't we meet at the

Lea Ann W. Hall

outside south entrance?" Glen glanced at his watch. "Say about 4:30, and I'll show you around a little."

"Might as well," was Ernie's unenthusiastic response.

"Then we'll go eat somewhere, so the energy spent won't be a total waste of time. How does Hacienda sound?"

"You're on! See ya at 4:30."

As he hung up, Glen mused that he was glad he'd been able to recall where Ernie's favorite eating spot was during last softball season. Now all he had to do was remember what he'd done with the CMCC key to the coaches' office, since May was definitely during the off-season. He hoped he'd just left it on his key ring. He checked and blew a sigh of relief. It was there, and so was the key to the equipment room.

Glen and Ernie entered the CMCC at the south end. When they arrived where the short hallway led back to the equipment room, Glen halted and looked toward the closed door. "Do you want to look in there?"

Ernie grimaced but said, "Might as well."

They scouted around among the football equipment and supplies, which had been moved to the back to make room for baseball gear. They saw nothing out of the ordinary. Both noticed the two oblong windows with frosted panes, high in one wall.

Ernie commented as they were leaving the room. "What about the door lock Brett mentioned?" Ernie asked, noting that a lock was not visible on the inside doorknob.

"I had it replaced. There was no earthly reason to have a lock that could be triggered from inside anyway. Now, even when the door's locked from the outside, you can just turn the knob and walk out. No one can get locked in, accidentally or otherwise."

"Want to try it?" Glen asked, handing Ernie the keys and

ThreadBare

stepping back into the room. "It's the one which says Lock Master on it," he added as he closed the door between them. He could hear Ernie fumbling with the keys and shoving one into the keyhole below the doorknob. Then he heard a distinct click. "Did you get it locked?" he hollered.

Ernie started twisting the outer doorknob. Glen watched as the inner doorknob shifted slightly back and forth, but the door remained securely locked. "Are you ready for the magic? Then stand clear," Glen warned as he turned the inside knob, swung the door back and stepped out into the short hallway. As Glen took the keys and unlocked the door, Ernie asked him if the locksmith had taken the old lock with him. "Nope, I stuck it in a drawer," he replied.

Back in the office area, Glen squatted to open the bottom drawer of a tall, metal filing cabinet. He reached clear to the back of it and tossed a used door lock assembly up to Ernie. "Want to take a look?" Ernie studied and probed it with his hands and his mind.

Glen explained, "You see, the inside knob works just like the lock on the bathroom door in my apartment. When you want to lock it, you turn that flange-like gismo in the center of the knob from horizontal to vertical, and you know the door is locked. You can't even turn the knob from the inside. I oughta know about that. I've conked my forehead a couple of times when I was in the bathroom and had company and forgot that I'd locked the dumb door."

Glen proceeded to carry out the instructions he'd just given. "Then to get the door unlocked, you have to turn the gismo back to horizontal, like this." The assembly made a distinct clunk. "That's what I hate about the one at home, too. Company can hear me unlocking the door, and it's like announcing to them that I don't trust them or something."

Glen's little confession made Ernie start to snicker.

Then, as he thought more about it, he began to laugh aloud, until he saw the scowl on Glen's face.

"I'm glad you found that so amusing."

"Sorry, it just struck me funny." No longer able to suppress his glee, Ernie clapped his hands together and chortled. "Yeah, man, I may have to use that one to blackmail you."

After putting the old assembly back in the file drawer, Glen sat down at his desk, tossed his keys on top of it, propped up his feet, and waited impatiently until Ernie's gales of laughter subsided somewhat, then asked, "Are you quite through?"

"I think so," Ernie replied, wiping his eyes with his thumb and index finger while trying hard to keep the corners of his mouth from turning up.

"I thought maybe you were freaking out."

"So did I, man. It felt great!" Ernie exulted, relaxing and leaning his rump against Glen's desk. "Sure beats being grumpy."

Glen gripped the desk and yanked it just enough to knock Ernie off balance. "Do you plan to do this again while we're eating dinner tonight, in a public place?"

Regaining his balance, Ernie turned around and asked, "Would it embarrass you if I did?"

"Heck, no. I'd just ask to be moved to another table and pretend that I didn't know the laughing hyena."

That almost set Ernie off again. Perhaps he was on the verge of hysteria.

Glen got up from behind his desk, picking up his keys. "Is there anything else in here that you think you should check out?"

As Ernie's gaze moved slowly around the room, he shrugged. Then his gaze returned to admire the row of trophies, which lined the top of a bank of filing cabinets.

They were beauties, and all six of them looked identical. He stepped closer. On top was an imposing shiny figure, a passer with his elbow drawn back to fire the ball, both feet planted solidly on the large block of handsome walnut which formed the base of each trophy. On the front of each block was a small plate bearing the year of the award. The dates ran from 1990 through 1994. Then the shiniest one was dated 1996.

"I thought this team had won seven consecutive championships, more than any other team in the history of small fry football in the state of Missouri," Ernie commented thoughtfully.

"Right on. I wasn't sure I could maintain that tradition last season. But we did it, thanks to some of our speedy players. The opposition just couldn't keep up with our ball carriers. Actually that passer up there," Glen pointed out as he approached the 1996 trophy, "is kind of misrepresentative of last year's team. In one game, we did not even throw a single pass. It's not worth the risks, when you can just sweep the ends or slant off-tackle for five-plus yards per carry."

"So where's the seventh trophy? The one for 1995 seems to be missing."

"Missing?" Glen echoed, dumbfounded. When he'd inherited the job, he'd never bothered to take an inventory of the trophies. Quickly, he began counting passers and checking dates.

Ernie's eyes were drawn back to the first of the trophies and slid from the magnificent passer down to the polished wooden base. The 1990 date hit Ernie between the eyes. He grabbed Glen's shoulder, gripping it so hard that Glen winced, even his eyes stung with shooting darts of pain. Instinctively, Glen wrenched himself loose and assumed a guarded, defensive stance, shouting, "What are you trying to do, break my shoulder blade or my collarbone?"

"Look at this!" Ernie demanded, jabbing his index finger accusingly at the 1990 trophy. Glen eyed Ernie warily before forcing himself to focus on the emblem Ernie was pointing at. "Remember those burned pieces of metal I showed you from Macklin's barbecue pit? Tell me this isn't the same kind of date plate."

When Glen stepped closer, recognition altered his expression to one of horrified awe. He turned toward Ernie.

"1995," they whispered in unison.

Glen's voice was stricken as he said, "That scum bug burned up the murder weapon."

"Then where's the passer? It wouldn't have melted completely in a fire like that. The heat intensity wouldn't have been high enough," Ernie observed.

The two friends stared at each other for a long moment. And Ernie could hear Chief Kinard's words about nothing seeming to be what it really is. Who would have benefited from Phil Vincent's death? Macklin? Maybe, to keep him quiet. Beth Vincent? Possibly, to live off his wealth. Or possibly, for the sake of a lover. But wouldn't that mysterious lover have surfaced by now, if there were one? Or had she just paid off a hit man?

What about Macklin's wife? Could Macklin have phoned her and told her about his encounter with Vincent, and then she took it upon herself to silence Vincent to protect her husband and his untarnished reputation? Or maybe she was just Macklin's accomplice.

What about the man standing in front of me? Glen Knox? Preposterous! What did he have to gain? Surely, one does not join a conspiracy to kill, in hopes of moving closer to a top coaching job in the little leagues. Surely not.

"What are you going to do now," Glen inquired, watching Ernie intently, "tell Chief Kinard?"

"Whatever we've discovered here can wait until morning. Right now, my friend, it's time to go get some tacos and chalupas." While they were at Hacienda, Ernie excused himself to go make a phone call. It was to connect him to the police station and have a tail put on Knox. Just as a precautionary move. Ridiculous though it might seem, the move could help to clear Knox, if it didn't end up helping to convict him of a crime.

Chapter 22

ERNIE LEARNED SOMETHING new about his boss every other week, it seemed. June proved to be no exception. Regarding the Vincent case, he'd brought the chief up to date on his research, his talks with the Vincents and Coach Knox, and the coroner's verification that the dimensions of the base of the 1990 trophy (which Glen had allowed Ernie to borrow) matched the photos of Phil Vincent's temple wound.

No sooner had Ernie finished the report from the coroner, than Chief Kinard picked up his phone and began making arrangements to go question Macklin in the penitentiary. He instructed Ernie that he was to go, too, and do the driving.

Then he explained that he planned to confront Macklin about the missing trophy, the recovered burnt pieces of metal, and the recent coroner's statement. If that didn't bring a confession, and it became necessary to tighten the screws on Macklin, the chief said they'd try a different approach. Ernie thought to himself, like what? He was starting to ask that very question when a call came in to the chief, who nodded to Ernie and gave him a curt wave of dismissal. It must have been Mrs. Kinard.

On the way to the penitentiary, the chief had fallen

asleep before Ernie finished backing the police cruiser out of its designated space and its tailpipe cleared the parking lot. Ernie shrugged and told himself that maybe Macklin would crack, and it wouldn't be necessary to come up with "a different approach," whatever that might be.

Ernie felt himself tensing as Macklin was led into a small, plain room by two guards. The chief was seated on one side of a large, metal table and Ernie sat at one end. Macklin plopped himself in the seat directly across from Chief Kinard. There was an air of defeat about the prisoner, and yet somehow he seemed self-assured. Was it possible to be smug in defeat?

Macklin didn't crack, despite the indisputable motive and evidence. Again his hazel eyes spewed green sparks. And when Chief Kinard asked who might have been burning a murder weapon in Macklin's backyard, the defiant prisoner made a smart remark about it must have been the Easter Bunny. The chief was not amused. He told Macklin that the only other person he could think of logically who would be doing such a thing had to be Mrs. Macklin. Now the chief had the man's full attention. Ernie could feel Macklin's hatred heating the room.

His eyes riveted deadly holes in the chief's face, and he hissed that his wife better be left out of this. While Ernie waited as the hair on the back of his neck settled back in place, Chief Kinard just sat there calmly, folded his thick arms, and blinked at Macklin several times. Then the chief asked Macklin if he could come up with any likely suspects, OTHER than the Easter Bunny, himself . . . or his wife.

Lunging across the table at Chief Kinard, Macklin quickly reseated himself when the two guards moved in from respective corners of the room, each brandishing a truncheon. Then Macklin's green eyes focused again on the chief and resumed puncturing his face. Spitting out words,

Macklin said his wife had suffered dearly already, that she was a God-fearing woman, a wonderful mother, and that she didn't deserve any of this.

Ernie was so tense, after being on the brink of pinning Macklin to the table when the former coach had dived for the chief, that his own body didn't seem to be touching any part of the chair on which he was sitting.

The chief went on to explain that he believed the D.A. would be willing to go along with bringing Mrs. Macklin to trial, especially when presented with a phone record which showed that Macklin had placed a brief call from the CMCC to his home within a half hour after Brett Cardell had fled on his bike. Macklin insisted that he called her only to tell her he wouldn't be able to make it home for dinner.

When Chief Kinard asked why not, Macklin had started to say he'd had a late appointment. Then he realized he didn't have anyone to verify that, because his appointment had been with a good friend, out on old Bonhomme Road, but a friend quite dead and unable to testify on Macklin's behalf.

"Phil couldn't leave it alone. He just couldn't let it be!"

Rocking back and forth in his chair, bitter resignation mingling with nervous relief, Macklin viciously snarled the words that were music to Chief Kinard's ears, "Where do I sign the damn thing?"

Chapter 23

AS ERNIE DROVE back home, the chief didn't sleep this time. Instead, he spent a lot of time looking at the wooded Missouri hillsides and the limestone bluffs. Still stunned, Ernie too was silent.

As they neared the outskirts of St. Louis and turned off the interstate, Ernie finally mustered up enough moxie to ask the chief how he knew he could push the right button by accusing Macklin's wife. Smiling sadly, he explained that Joyce Macklin and his own wife had played cards in the same bridge club for countless years. The chief's wife knew her very well.

So the chief knew Mrs. Macklin was a kind, decent, fun-loving, upstanding, church-going woman, who deeply loved her family. She was enjoying her life immensely—a wonderful marriage to a fine, successful man and the additional blessings of two healthy, young children.

The chief went on to explain that Martin Macklin had started his own construction company and served his community in many ways, including the construction of several play areas in neighborhood parks at his own expense. He was also the sponsor and coach of a football team of youngsters with whom he had worked most effectively for more than a decade.

Looking over at Ernie, the chief concluded, "I didn't think he'd hide behind his wife on this, and completely destroy their family by risking her conviction for a murder that he himself had committed. I guess I was banking on him having a few shreds of decency left in him."

As they pulled into the police parking lot, the chief asked Ernie if he had time to break the news to the Vincents or should he phone them himself. Ernie said he'd take care of it. But he knew it wouldn't be by means of a phone call.

Chapter 24

WHEN ERNIE PULLED up in front of the Vincent home, it was nearly dark. A damp chill, a little unusual for early June, pervaded the air. As he turned off his headlights, he saw the Vincents' two-car garage light come on and the overhead door began to rise. Beth's dark green minivan, headlights and back-up lights on, began to roll down the driveway while the overhead door lowered itself again. Then her brake lights flashed on. Beth had noticed the cruiser. Ernie got out and strode over to her side of the van as she lowered her window.

"It looks like you're on your way out. I can come back another time."

Beth studied his face in the deep twilight and said, "No, I was just going to pick up something at the grocery store, but that can wait."

She tapped the garage door's remote opener, raising the door and relighting the garage. She then drove back up the drive and pulled into the garage. Hesitantly, Ernie made his way up the driveway. Getting out of the van, Beth waited at the door to the kitchen until Ernie was clear of the overhead door before pressing the remote button on the garage wall.

He heard the door sliding closed behind him and felt his instincts warning him. But now he knew she in no way had been involved in her husband's murder, so he let his heart lead him on. While she was putting her car keys back in her purse, he opened the door for her, then followed her in. She paused to flip on a light switch. Then he swung the door closed behind them.

"Nan around?" Ernie queried.

"She left for Minnesota two days ago."

"I bet it's quiet here without her around."

"It is," Beth sighed. "But I have my friends, and I've started volunteering at St. Luke's twice a week." Her voice lifted as she added, "They're thinking about letting me work in the emergency room."

"Really! You think you'd like that?"

"Oh, yes, I was finishing my nurse's training when I met Phil, who was finishing up his law degree."

"I didn't realize that."

Beth sensed that it was time to change the subject. "Coffee?"

"Decaf?" he asked, exactly on cue.

"Right." He could hear the smile in her voice as she stood on tiptoe and pulled two large mugs from the second shelf of the cupboard. She was wearing trim black slacks and a royal blue cardigan with a matching pullover beneath it.

He slipped off his jacket and draped it around the back of one of the kitchen chairs, then eased himself into another chair. Meanwhile, Beth pressed the switch for the light suspended over the breakfast table. Its large mosaic of colored glass panels lent a colorful glow to the room. After pouring the coffee, she handed Ernie a mug, and sat down across from him. She had not removed her cardigan, and her slender fingers were wrapped around her mug, seeking its warmth. Her wedding ring still glinted on her left hand.

"It's been a long day," Ernie commented.

"I'm sure that's what you came here to say." This time he could see as well as hear her soft smile.

Quietly he began to speak, reading a myriad of expressions that flitted across her lovely face as he started relating the events of the day. Taking a deep breath, he continued. "Then Chief Kinard decided we had enough evidence to make a trip to the pen today to see Martin Macklin." He noticed the troubled frown that appeared on Beth's brow but hastened on. "I know that what I am going to say next will come as a shock to you, but you need to know." Beth was holding her breath. "Macklin confessed to killing your husband."

Closing her eyes and lowering her head, Beth began to rub her fingertips up and down her brow, in the small space between her bangs and her nose. "But why?" she murmured. "They were such good friends."

"Your husband discovered what Macklin was doing to Brett Cardell."

"I don't understand. I thought Coach Knox did that." Then her head came up, eyes wide open. her hands dropping limply to the table. "Oh, my God! You mean Phil didn't just check the schedule and head for home like Coach Macklin said he did?"

"No, he didn't," Ernie replied quietly.

"That man lied and kept up that lie for a year and a half? Even to my own face! What kind of person would do such a thing?" Ernie just shook his head.

"What happened? You said Phil died from a blow to the head. Coach Macklin clubbed him with something?"

"It was a trophy, right there in the CMCC," Ernie said, but she was staring off somewhere over his head.

"He must have hit Phil when he wasn't even looking! But

why? Because Phil found out about Brett? That's no reason to kill a friend."

"It is, if your friend refuses to turn his head and let things go on as before, because he believes in protecting a young boy above anything else." Beth closed her eyes again, and the tears came. "Your husband was going to knock down Macklin's house of cards and put him away, and Macklin couldn't let that happen without trying to stop him."

Beth was looking across the table at Ernie now, with weary anger in her brimming eyes. "You didn't even know Phil. He wasn't a fighter. He always talked his way out of tough situations."

"Apparently, Macklin was beyond words. He wouldn't let Phil near the phone. Indeed there was a fight. And according to Macklin, as he grabbed and swung that trophy, your husband was delivering a knockout punch that Macklin knew would have rendered him unconscious. And Macklin's guilt would have become public knowledge."

"What a waste!" Beth sobbed, burying her face in her folded arms on the table. "What a terrible, senseless waste." After a few moments, she stumbled away from the table to look blindly out the window above the kitchen sink. Tears ran in rivulets down her face as she rocked to and fro, with her fists clenched tightly to her chest just below her throat. Now and then, her body was wracked with enormous sobs.

Ernie had come around the table toward her. The ache in his chest was crowding his ability to breathe. How could he ease the pain of this suffering woman? Gently he cupped his hands against her shoulders, wondering if he should wrap his arms around her. His voice sounded hoarse as he told her, "At least your husband died for something he believed in. A lot of men who die early never get that chance."

She turned and burrowed her face into his shoulder.

He could feel her warm tears through his shirt. He found himself trying to soothe her by softly rubbing her back and patting her head like she was a kid sister. Finally she grew calm enough to pull a tissue from the pocket of her slacks and wipe her face.

Then she retrieved the two mugs and poured the coffee from them into the sink, saying it must be too cool to drink by now. As she refilled the cups, Ernie tried to tell her that wasn't necessary, but she insisted it was. Then he realized she did not want to be left alone. They sat back down at the table and talked about the weather and sports and had just started a discussion of national politics when she laughed at some dumb comment he made. She seemed much better, although her face was still splotchy. He thought he should leave now.

Standing up, Ernie said, "You can tell Nan the gist of what's happened. It will be better for her to hear it from her mother instead of me anyway."

Beth murmured, "There's still a lot I don't understand."

"I know. There are some details yet to be uncovered, but the majority of the puzzle has been filled in." He reached over and lifted his jacket from the back of its chair. As she led him to the front door, he promised, "I will let you know more details as we uncover them."

"I hope so. But what will you do when the last piece of the puzzle is in place?

He looked down at her lightly splotched face, trying to read those clear brown eyes, rimmed in red. "Do?"

"You know, this has almost become a habit. You'll at least have to drop by for coffee now and then."

He replied too quickly, "You can count on that." He knew he was grinning foolishly.

"Nan will want to see you, too. She'll be back August

4th. Did you know that from her pick of colleges across the country, she decided on Washington University, right here in St. Louis? Isn't that amazing? I know she'll be sorry when she hears that she missed seeing you tonight. You've become a special person in her life, you know."

Although what she'd revealed about Nan's feelings for him struck a mutually responsive chord in his heart, Ernie yearned to ask Beth if he meant anything to her, deep down in her own life. Instead, he nodded and left.

When he opened the driver's door of his cruiser, he realized he was still carrying his jacket and was shivering. "You idiot!" he muttered as he swung each arm into the jacket, slid into the seat, and took off. At least he'd remembered to turn on the headlights and hadn't locked himself out of the cruiser. He glanced into the rearview mirror. Well, wonder of wonders, his head was still on straight. Or was it?

Two blocks down the street, he pulled over and shifted the cruiser into Park. It was time for a talk with the idiot. He explained to himself that this kind of relationship could never work. It had no future. They couldn't keep chatting over coffee forever. He wanted either something more or nothing at all.

What more could there be? She was a well-to-do widow, whose close circle of friends consisted of wealthy and prominent people in the business and professional world. He was from a blue-collar family and proud of it. But she'd be dissatisfied with his world, and he'd be a misfit in hers. End of story.

Besides, other than as a kind police officer, she probably viewed him as someone she found amusing and entertaining, like a new pet. That he would never be, not for anyone, not even Beth. Okay, buddy, he told himself. I'm glad we got that straight. From here on, it's strictly professional.

Chapter 25

ERNIE WROTE UP some informal notes which he planned to take to the Vincents in mid-August after Nan's return home. The notes would help them put the missing puzzle pieces into place. Although he and the chief had watched the actual videotape of Macklin's confession, for the Vincent women, Ernie planned to sketch in what had happened, without getting too graphic.

During the taping, Macklin's voice and face had revealed the entire gamut of emotions. Starting slowly, he said that after Brett left, he and Coach Vincent went back inside the CMCC. But Phil kept after him. He insisted that he had seen the fifty-dollar bill as plain as day and had also heard the lock when Macklin opened the equipment room door. He even went so far as to go over and test the door's lock a couple of times, making it clunk each time. Then he spun on Macklin with fire in his deep blue eyes and said, "You're so clever with words! How do you intend to explain away the lock? The same way you lied about the money?"

"You're hearing things. Maybe both your sight and hearing are going bad." Macklin knew it was not a convincing response.

As they went on toward the coaches' office, Macklin

asked Phil what he was doing there today anyway. Phil laughed shortly and retorted, "That's a good one! You really want to know why I dropped by? Remember how often you've complimented me on this Snoopy tie and said you hadn't been able to find one like it? Well, I was a couple of miles from here for a meeting this afternoon. The meeting got kind of boring, and I started thinking about how much you like this tie. So I told myself, when I leave here, I'm going to surprise Marty and put this tie in his locker over at the CMCC. Then I'll surprise my gals, too. For the first time in eons, I'll go on home early, like I'd promised them this morning. But no, it looks like I got the biggest surprise of all!"

Marty tried to tell his friend that he was making a big deal out of nothing. As Phil glowered at Marty with steely blue eyes and a grieving heart, Marty sat down at the desk and tried to reason with him. "There's nothing to worry about. Look, this situation isn't as bad as it seems to you." His green eyes looked up at Phil beseechingly.

Phil turned his back on Marty, stating flatly, "I don't want to hear about it. You'll have to turn yourself in. There's no other choice." Turning back to look down at Macklin, Phil insisted, "Face the truth! You can't hide from it!"

"Listen, you don't understand! This is a win-win situation. The kid's getting good money. His parents don't know anything. I get what I want. And nobody's upset, except you!"

Marty could not bring himself to look his friend in the face, but he saw Phil's sports coat expanding and could sense Phil's growing hostility. In a tightly controlled voice, Phil said, "Either you call the police now, or I'll pick up the phone myself."

"Leave this alone, man!" Marty spat, using both his hands to smooth his sun-streaked hair back from his forehead with rough, desperate strokes. His pinstriped shirt was pulling almost to the point of escape from the sides of his belted khakis. "Just leave it alone!"

Then Phil pivoted, challenging Marty by reaching for the phone. Marty knocked the phone off the desk with a sweep of his arm and ducked out of the chair. Reaching out instinctively with his right hand, he grabbed a hammer that lay on the bottom shelf of a utility cart next to the desk. Although both men were physically fit, Marty felt stronger as he crouched with the hammer in his hand. He knew Phil Vincent had done well not only as a pass receiver but also as a boxer during his college days. He realized, too, that his adversary had a much longer arm reach than he had. But most of all, he was acutely aware that this contest was not going to be for the sport of it.

Phil had intended to pull the phone over, dial the police station, and hand the receiver to Marty. Livid now, he lunged at Marty in a flash, jamming his knee into Marty's chest and knocking the breath out of him. Phil's lightning takedown stunned Marty. The long fingers on one of Phil's hands were clutching the middle of Marty's right forearm. And his other hand seized Marty's right arm above the elbow. Marty shoved his free arm with all his might against Phil's chest and tried to twist his right arm enough to take a swing at Phil with the hammer. But Phil was pounding Marty's arm against the edge of the desk, again and again, shooting shock waves of pain from Marty's shoulder to his fingertips.

Marty slammed his left arm and fist at Phil again, this time finding Phil's unguarded stomach and feeling the gouge that Phil's buckle made up through the fleshy underside of his thumb and deep into his wrist. Phil stumbled to his knees, throwing Marty off balance, because Phil still had not loosened his grip on Marty's arm. He kept on, bashing Marty's elbow against the desk's edge over and over and causing a numbness so overpowering that Marty finally lost his grip, and the hammer clattered to the concrete floor.

Rising to step on the hammer's handle with one foot, Phil released his two-handed grip on Marty's arm. As he rose to his full height, he shook his shoulders to straighten his sports coat while he smoothed down his tie and ran his hand across his forehead to shove his disheveled auburn hair to one side. "Don't you ever—"

Leading with a shoulder, Marty threw his full weight against Phil's chest, driving him across the cramped room and into the bank of filing cabinets. Then Marty felt a sharp jab to his ribs, which doubled him over. Another jab on the other side of his ribs nearly lifted him off his feet and forced a groan from between his teeth. He knew what was coming next, an upper cut to his chin—and he'd be out cold. Then Phil would pick up the phone, and it would be all over.

Marty spun away from Phil, along the cabinets, backing against them for defense. Phil came after him, fury blazing from his eyes and fists doubled. Desperately, Marty flung his right arm back on top the cabinets in an attempt to find something with which to protect himself. He sent a stapler skittering across the concrete floor, and several jostled papers fluttered downward as Phil sent a punishing jab under Marty's guarding left arm and into his midsection. Gasping to find a way to breathe, Marty felt a cool metal object against his groping right hand. He gripped hard and swung with all his might, just as Phil's uppercut jarred Marty's teeth then slid off harmlessly.

Phil crumpled from the blow, which had caught him just above his left ear. The wooden base of the trophy tumbled away from Phil's body, while Marty still held the passer upside down in his shaking hand. It wasn't just his hands that were shaking. His whole body was trembling, and his hazel eyes had lost their fire. He knelt down feebly to take the pulse in Phil's neck and knew he wouldn't find one.

Then, being the pragmatist that he was, he set the phone back on the desk and put the receiver in its cradle momentarily before lifting it again to see if the phone still worked. Hearing the dial tone, he called his wife to say he wouldn't be home for dinner.

Chapter 26

WHEN ERNIE ARRIVED at the Vincent home, he kidded a little with Nan as he sat down on the sofa and she plopped in the middle of the carpet. She was wearing a baggy, forest green sweatshirt that would have been roomy, even on him. He wondered if it had belonged to her dad. The deep color set off the reddish tint of her thick, straight hair and seemed to enhance the dark blue of her eyes. Beth sat in her cozy chair, and he avoided looking at her other than briefly and professionally. He concentrated on the notepad in his hand and started out by explaining what had happened after Brett fled on his bike.

Ernie went on to explain how Macklin had mopped up the blood with towels and had waited for total darkness while he decided what to do with Phil's body. Ernie didn't add how that also had given him time to arrange Phil's body for later.

Marty had immediately begun silently praying that no one would show up before he could dispose of Phil's body. He worried about someone spotting Phil's Camaro. At least Phil had parked the black car in the back lot, where it was less conspicuous. Marty decided to leave Phil's legs bent where he'd gone down, but turned his head so that the wounded side was cradled in a couple of thickly folded white towels. With the right side of Phil's face and head untouched, he looked like he might have had a heart attack. Marty also stretched out Phil's right arm and then crooked the elbow some. That position should work when Marty transferred Phil to the back seat of his Lincoln, to keep him from rolling onto the floor whenever Marty applied the brakes.

Then, under cover of darkness, Macklin placed a new pillow of towels on the plush back seat of his car and successfully lugged Phil's body to the big Lincoln. To any sharp-eyed trucker who might pull up beside them at a traffic light, Phil would look blissfully asleep in the back of Marty's car.

Wrestling Phil's dead weight into the car had been tough, especially after all the punishment his own body had taken from Phil's fists. He'd had to open the back door behind the driver's side and prop Phil's head and shoulders against the frame. Then he's gone to the other back door, crawled across to where his dead friend rested, grabbed him under the armpits, dragged him across the back seat, and arranged him in peaceful sleep.

Ever the pragmatist, Marty managed to keep everything in perspective and did not allow himself to break down emotionally during the entire ordeal. He had even had the presence of mind to remember to find Phil's car keys just before he dragged Phil's body from the Lincoln onto Old Bonhomme Road.

With his brain working in survival mode, Macklin had carefully analyzed every detail as he set up his plan to create a crime scene far from Kirkwood and to leave the CMCC looking as normal as it would on any other day.

First, he dealt with the set of bloodied towels, rinsing them twice and wringing them out while the sun was going down, and then hanging them in the shower room to dry.

After he returned from his road trip, the towels were still damp when he gathered them up with the barely bloodied ones from the car and took them home with him, in the cardboard box that also held the base of the broken trophy. He'd take them out of the car trunk tomorrow night and burn them in his brick barbecue pit, box and all, stirring them with a poker until not a shred was left.

Marty knew he'd made a wise decision when he elected not to try to cram his friend's large frame into the trunk. Besides, this way, the detectives wouldn't be able to find anything suspicious on Phil's clothes, like fibers or other substances traceable to his trunk.

And if for some unimaginable reason, his car would ever be inspected by the police, they wouldn't find unexplainable clothing fibers or hair from Phil inside the trunk. And anything of that nature on the interior of Marty's car would not be suspicious. After all, Phil Vincent had ridden in his car many times, although only Marty knew Phil had never been in the back seat before.

Chapter 27

NOW, ALTHOUGH ERNIE had not given them all the details, Nan and Beth understood the strange circumstances that had surrounded Phil's death -- why the hit-and-run version made no sense. Although, to a large extent, this version didn't make any real sense either. But at least the puzzle pieces were all in place . . . mostly.

Ernie couldn't bring himself to lift his eyes from his notepad. Then he heard Nan's tremulous voice asking, "What about the Camaro? Was it Macklin who drove it to Illinois and burned it?"

Ernie nodded. "When Macklin returned from Old Bonhomme Road to the CMCC parking lot, he knew he had to get rid of your dad's car. At first, he said he thought he'd just park it at your dad's law office. So he started driving toward downtown. But then he realized he didn't know enough about that situation. He wasn't sure if your dad had a reserved parking place or if a security guard would be on duty. So he drove the Camaro over the Eads Bridge, up to an old rock quarry on the Illinois side, and set it afire."

"What happened to the passer that broke off of the trophy?" Nan asked him. A single tear lay against one finely freckled cheek. Her eyes glistened, but she looked steadily at him, with inner strength.

"Macklin said he walked down to the Mississippi, which is three or four miles from the quarry, and threw it in the river before he went back to the CMCC. It may never be recovered."

"How did he get back without a car?"

She would make one smashing lawyer someday, Ernie thought to himself, if that is what she chose to be.

"He told us he walked to the MetroLink station in East St. Louis. He thought he might attract attention if he walked from the Illinois side back across one of the bridges. So he took the MetroLink and rode it back across Eads Bridge and clear out through downtown, to Forest Park. From there he walked a mile on, to the intersection of Skinker and Clayton Road, where he called a cab from a 24-hour service station."

"It seems like it would have been a lot easier for him just to get off at one of the earlier MetroLink stations, call Mrs. Macklin, and have her come in the Mustang and get him at Busch Stadium, or the Kiel Center, or Union Station. Wherever he was calling from. Then she could just pick him up and take him to get his car at the CMCC," Nan observed.

"True. But strange as it might seem, he did not want to implicate her in any way."

The three of them exchanged wordless glances. The room, for all its bright color, was very somber, as though canopied by a dark cloud.

Ernie got to his feet, stifling the urge to stretch. Nan followed him to the door like a faithful puppy, while Beth remained in her chair. As he opened the door, Ernie heard Nan ask, "What about the tie?"

He turned to face the young woman. "The tie? Oh, the Snoopy tie."

She nodded.

"Macklin told us that he decided, while he was waiting for darkness to fall, to keep your dad's tie. He explained that he knew your dad had wanted him to have it, and to him it seemed fitting that he should remove it and take it home with him. Besides, he reasoned that there was no way anyone could prove that particular tie belonged to your dad. He never dreamed he'd ever be questioned in earnest about the tie, let alone that there were some small but identifiable stitches of pink thread in the label.

"Maybe if he'd undone the knot on that Snoopy tie when he hung it up, he might have noticed the pink stitching sometime when he was retying the knot. I don't know whether that would have kept him from wearing it or not. He's a hard read."

Ernie gazed out the door for a moment, watching a squirrel burrowing in the yard. Then he continued. "When the police first began interrogating him about the tie, it was simple for him when he decided to confirm that your dad dropped by the CMCC and told Marty he wanted him to have the tie." Ernie glanced outside again, but the squirrel had scurried away.

Suddenly, he turned and looked at Nan. "Would you like to have that tie back? When this trial is over and after it has been thoroughly photographed, I will see that you get it back."

Nan slipped her hand into his and said simply, "Thanks, Ernie," then squeezed his hand and released it.

Surprised and deeply moved, Ernie glanced toward Beth's chair but was interrupted by her cola eyes staring at him from a couple of feet away. He hadn't heard her approach them. He didn't even know how long she had been standing there, looking so small and vulnerable.

Ernie looked evenly at Nan and said, "You've never called me Ernie before."

Nan shrugged and said, "Oh, that's what Mom calls you all the time."

Ernie expected a quick denial, but Beth just lowered her eyes, bit her lower lip, and said nothing. He noticed that she was still wearing her wedding ring

Ernie nodded and left. It seemed like the best thing he did around the Vincent household was to nod and leave. Beth had not actually said anything to him, but he could read a great deal in her behavior. Or so he thought. Was he imagining things? Usually he had an instinctive way of reading people. But that was when he was not emotionally involved. In this case, he hadn't kept his guard up the way he should have. Gotta keep it professional, Ernie told himself as he drove away. That should be easy to do, at least until the trial started.

Meanwhile, Beth drew her peaked eyebrows together and gave her daughter one of those thundercloud looks, as a belated reaction to Nan's slip of the tongue. Nan chose to ignore her mom's expression, feeling that although her comment had been careless, it might also have been a good thing for Ernie to hear.

Then Nan rested her arm lightly across her mother's shoulders as they stood together in the doorway. Beth slipped her arm around her daughter's waist as Nan tipped her auburn head against the top of her mother's dark one. And they watched the cruiser until it disappeared from sight.

Chapter 28

THE NEXT MORNING, while Nan was putting the breakfast dishes into the dishwasher, Beth wiped the kitchen counters down and paused as she looked at Nan, "Since Ernie has treated us so well, I feel like we should somehow show our appreciation."

"Hmmm, sending flowers does not seem right," Nan pondered. "How about a gift card to a nice restaurant? Wait, no!

Aren't you going to see the Cards play tomorrow night?"

What does that have to do with thinking of something for Ernie? Oh, you mean I could see if he wants to go to the game?"

"Very good, Mom!"

Gazing seriously at her daughter, Beth said, "Since it would be kind of a last minute, casual thing, and he loves sports, I think that just might work. If it turns out that he can't make it, we will have to come up with something else."

With her mustered courage, Beth went straight to the phone and called Ernie, who was at his desk, trying to tie up some loose ends and bring a bit of organization to his day.

"Ernie, it's Beth Vincent. Some of my friends are going

to the Cardinal game tomorrow evening. Would you be interested in going with us?"

He didn't breathe while he thought of what he should say.

Nan took the phone gently from her mother and offered more information. "Hi, Ernie! The husband of one of Mom's friends in the garden club owns a company that has a luxury box at Busch Stadium. It's a pretty good set-up."

"Are you going?"

"With a bunch of middle-aged people? I don't think so! Here's Mom again"

How did this girl always manage to make him laugh?

Re-gathering his thoughts, he rationalized that this was no big deal, and I may never get another opportunity to sit in one of those boxes. So when Beth repeated her invitation to see the game, he heard his voice saying, "Sure, why not."

Beth said, "Since you're the guest, I can drive."

Ernie replied that since he was the guest, the least he could do was drive. He also explained that it wouldn't be the cruiser, because he did have his own car that he drove off-duty.

"Do you like to watch batting practice?"

"Of course."

"Then we better leave about 5:45, Ernie. Oh, and there'll be plenty to eat at the ballpark. Stan always puts on quite a spread."

"Stan the Man Musial?" Ernie asked, Beth heard his voice and knew that he had a twinkle in his eyes.

"No, not hardly," Beth laughed. "Stan Davidson. He owns the electronics company."

"See you at 5:45 tomorrow?"

"I'll be ready."

After Beth hung up the phone, Nan couldn't resist singing, "Mom's got a date! Mom's got a date!"

ThreadBare

Beth finally gave up trying to shush her and every half hour or so, Nan would singsong again. Beth knew she should find Nan's prattling to be an irritation to her, but it wasn't. After all, this officer had done a lot for their family, and what better way to repay him.

Chapter 29

BATTING PRACTICE HAD been fun to watch, because Ernie and Beth had arrived ahead of the others. The usher had checked his list for their names, then had admitted them to the elite facility, complete with a half bath, a bar, a refrigerator, a microwave, and a closed-circuit large-screen TV. They had walked on through the air-conditioned portion of the box to sit outside, in front of the glassed-in space.

Ernie thought that was great, because they were close to first base and had a ceiling fan to keep the humid August air moving. But as others began to appear in the box, one of the wives slid the glass door open, popped her head out, and cooed for Beth to come inside out of the heat. So she and Ernie had gone inside, where the cooing wife showed her innocent amazement at learning that Beth's escort was a police officer, although she already knew this was the officer who had spent so much time trying to solve the mystery of Phil Vincent's death. What she'd really wanted was to get a good look at him. She truly was not disappointed.

Ernie found it hard to concentrate on the game. Most of the others, all casually but expensively well-attired, engaged him in shallow conversation for a few minutes. But they were all talking about people and places, which for the most part were unfamiliar to him. However, he was generously plied with hotdogs, chips, and peanuts. He even indulged in a couple of cold beers.

He felt like he blended in okay in his vertical thin-striped red, dark green, and navy shirt and casual navy slacks and was glad he'd decided against wearing jeans. He didn't want to embarrass Beth in any way. But he certainly could have worn a pair of walking shorts, because he would have looked a lot better than any of the three guys from the electronic company who were wearing them.

Behind the glass door, the ballgame had a remote quality about it, what with all the conversations going on. Ernie sat where he could keep an eye on the playing field. However, the large TV monitor was on a counter off to Ernie's right, so he had to turn his head if he wanted to see a close-up of what was going on.

Beth was sitting across from him, looking simple but chic in a lightweight lavender jump suit, with pearly gray buttons that matched her slightly larger earrings and her silver-gray flats. He was pleased that she was in his direct view, a reassuring sight. Their eyes met in a friendly way several times.

Most of the others were wrapped up in impressing each other with their images, experiences, and clever comments. Beth easily held her own, but with her it was natural, not phony. The only time anyone seemed to be paying attention to the game was when one of the guys would shout, "Take a look at this replay!"

Ernie had thought the seventh-inning stretch would never get here. Then Beth stepped over to him while everyone was standing up, slipped her dainty hand in his, and led him toward the exit door while explaining to Stan Davidson's wife

ThreadBare

that they'd had a wonderful time and that Ernie had an early shift in the morning.

As they descended the outside ramps that wrap the stadium, Beth let her hand slip out of his and said, "Now you're free. I forgot how stifling some of those people can be."

Ernie looked at her apologetically and asked, "Was I so transparent?"

She laughed, and as her eyes twinkled, she said, "I bet you've been transparent since the day you were born." He looked at her, but couldn't decipher what that remark meant. He was about to ask her, when she broke in with a suggestion.

"Let's go down and watch the end of the game from behind the seats on the lower level." So they did.

Ernie had a feeling that Beth had probably done something along these lines before, and that a tall attorney had been beside her then. Where they stood, a cool breeze caressed their backs. They were in a good position for leaving quickly when the game was over, and they were able to ensure that the Cards managed to hang on to their two-run lead through the top of the ninth, for a victory.

They headed for the parking garage immediately, but some of the crowd began to overtake them. The streams of foot traffic trying to move through each other, and the river-like one flowing through them and surging toward the pedestrian bridge, carried the crowds along into the press of the shifting flows. Ernie thought the situation made for a good excuse to clasp Beth's hand and do the blocking for her as they worked their way across the broad pedestrian bridge and through the jostling throngs.

As he drove expertly in the homebound traffic, Ernie commented. "If I'd have known you felt stifled, too, I'd have suggested we leave that lap of luxury even sooner than we did. But whenever that idea would cross my mind, I'd tell myself no, because I didn't want to make us a topic of gossip among your friends. I guess that's why I was kind of surprised at you getting us out of there in the middle of the seventh."

Beth chuckled. "Ernie, believe me, we will be a topic of gossip among my friends, even if we'd endured that box until the last out was made."

"I don't want to make it harder for you to move back into social life, Beth. That's the last thing in the world I want to do."

"You didn't. You made it easier, Ernie. See, with you around, most of the women were envious, and the guys all behaved themselves."

Ernie was silent the rest of the way. He wondered if he'd been used. Then he put it out of his head and tuned in some classical music on the radio. They should be able to listen to that without hearing any love songs, since it was all instrumental. Besides people who are just friends sure don't need to be listening to romantic music. He would give the possibility of being used by Beth more careful study after he got home tonight. On second thought, why bother?

Chapter 30

IT HAD BEEN three weeks since Ernie had seen Beth. He hadn't been able to determine in his mind if she had meant to use him or not. But he certainly wasn't going to set himself up again by initiating contact with her.

September came in rainy. Sipping his morning coffee, Ernie reared the front two legs of his chair a couple of inches off the floor and stared broodingly out the window. Was it something he'd said, or didn't say? Was he too brash in holding her hand all the way to the car? Did she think that wasn't enough? Had she expected more from him?

Now he was mad. That's why he'd finally quit letting friends set him up with anyone after his divorce. Dating was far too complex, too frustrating, and at times, downright demeaning. And this time, it was interfering with his work . . . he wasn't even dating her . . . not really.

Chapter 31

AFTER DINNER THAT night, he kept visualizing himself arriving at the Vincent home and walking up to the front door. What would Beth's expression be when she opened the door?

To get rid of the recurring scene, he picked up the local paper and began to read it thoroughly, page by page. He liked it better when he got over to where some of the pages had big display ads and not so much print. Then he turned the page and saw an ad for an event coming next week to the TransWorld Dome (which he thought should have a better name, like the "Show Me" Dome). It was a rodeo. That's what he needed, was to get out and do something that would be a real treat.

He'd call some of the guys, get something set up, and volunteer to get the tickets. But he just kept sitting there, holding the paper, and getting mad all over again. Finally he flung the newspaper on the floor.

I'm not going to get any sleep until I get things resolved with Beth once and for all, he told himself, still steaming. He knew he shouldn't pick up the phone when he was mad, but he wanted to get to the bottom of this. He'd memorized the number long ago.

When he heard a female voice on the other end of the line say, "Vincent residence," he asked, "Nan?" The voice replied no that this was her mother and could she take a message.

Then Ernie felt stupid and said, "You sound like your daughter."

"Is this Capt. Johnson?"

Capt. Johnson! So it had gone back to that, had it? "Yeah, Mrs. Vincent, you sound a lot like your daughter when you answer the phone."

He heard her tinkling laughter and could feel the redness in his face and the steam coming out of his ears.

"Oh, Ernie. I can always use a compliment like that, whether it's from one of Nan's beaus or you."

Now why had she switched back to Ernie? He wished she didn't confuse him so easily!

"So should I keep calling you Mrs. Vincent or go back to Beth?"

"Beth, of course! The only reason I addressed you so formally was on the chance that it might not really be you. I'd feel silly asking some stranger if he was Ernie. And if it was a stranger, I liked the idea of it sounding like I was expecting a call from a captain, be it an officer of the armed services or the police."

"Maybe you didn't think it was me because you were expecting someone else."

"Like who?"

"You tell me."

"What are you talking about?"

"Maybe one of your men friends."

"My men friends! Since when has that become a topic of discussion? Do I ever ask you about any of your women friends? I think not."

"You don't have to get huffy about it."

"Look who's the grumpy one." She was right on target with that one. "You asked to speak to Nan, and she really isn't here. She's moved back to the dorm for the fall semester. Do you want her number at Wash U?"

"Why would I be calling her?"

"Well, I suppose there could be a variety of reasons. Do you want me to guess until I come up with the right answer?"

This was getting out of hand, Ernie realized. And he didn't even know how it had all gotten started. "I was not calling Nan. I just thought it sounded like her voice." There was a slight pause.

"So why ARE you calling?"

"To see if you want to go to a rodeo." He couldn't believe he's just said that. How crazy could he be?

"A rodeo? That sounds like fun. Here in town?"

"No, in Cheyenne."

More tinkling laughter. "When does your jet leave?"

"In ten minutes." He heard himself chuckle. "Really, there's a national rodeo scheduled for the Dome next week."

"Any particular day?"

"Whatever works for you."

"How about Friday evening? Is it still on then?"

"Let me check." He rustled through the papers, trying to locate the blamed ad. Finally, he found it. "Friday's the last day. I'll call before they close this evening and order the tickets, if you want to go Friday."

"It's just that you don't have an early shift on Saturdays, do you? So we'd have more time than if we went on a week night."

Ernie felt a shiver up his spine that was usually reserved for special renditions of the "Star-Spangled Banner" or other momentous music. More time for what, he wondered.

"But," her voice floated on merrily, "if they're sold out for Friday, I can go any night of the week."

"I thought you have bridge club on Wednesday evenings."

"I do, but I could find someone to substitute for me." The receiver seemed to be trying to get away from him like a struggling catfish, if he didn't get a tight grip on it. "Should I buy a pair of western boots for this event?"

"That's not necessary," Ernie assured her.

"Will you be wearing boots?"

"Well, I do have a pair. Yeah, I guess so."

"But I won't look conspicuous if I don't wear boots?"

"No." He wanted to tell her that he'd take her even if she went bare-footed.

"Then let me know what we're going to be doing, cowboy."

He thought she knew what they were going to be doing. Then he understood what she was saying.

"I'll let you know what day and what time, et cetera."

"Okay, and thanks for thinking of me, Ernie. Bye-bye."

"Bye."

Thinking of her. That was an understatement! He immediately called and got pretty good tickets for Friday night. Then he called her right back to let her know that she wouldn't have to make any special arrangements regarding her bridge club.

When she started to say bye to his second call, he interrupted. "Mind if I ask you a question?"

"Go ahead."

"Where have you been the last three weeks?"

"I thought you'd had a pretty lousy time at the Cardinals game. You even clammed up after you turned on the radio while we were on the way home. So I felt like I had let you down. I guess I thought maybe you'd decided that I was too old for you or something."

That cut him to the quick. "Are you kidding? I'm sure you'll outlive me. Besides there are lots of women younger than you that might as well be older than you. Your mind can run circles around theirs." How much could he safely say? "You remind me of a teenager. And . . . and you are special in a way that will never grow old."

"Gee, I wish I had recorded that!"

"You'd like to use it to blackmail me someday, wouldn't you?"

"Maybe so, say about twenty years from now."

"By then, I'll probably be dead."

"Oh, Ernie, don't say such an awful thing!"

He felt contrite, wishing he hadn't made such a careless remark and longing to be there to comfort her.

After they hung up, while he was gathering and folding the scattered newspapers, a couple of thoughts occurred to him. One, in the form of a question, was: Would he be able to survive the roller coaster of emotions that Beth Vincent evoked in him? The other was the satisfied notion that he was for sure going to sleep soundly tonight.

Chapter 32

WHEN BETH TALKED to Nan on the phone, she told her daughter about going to the rodeo with Ernie and how it had been such a blast, to which Nan had retorted that her mom was catching on to the lingo. When Beth told her she'd even bought a pair of boots, Nan said maybe she needed to come home and help her mother shop for a western hat, so she could start line dancing, too. They both laughed at that.

Ernie and Beth had continued to see each other nearly every week clear up through Thanksgiving, carefully avoiding her circles of friends and his law enforcement associates, knowing that seemed to be the best way for the two of them to have a good time (or a blast).

During these times, they had developed what Beth considered to be a sweet tradition. When Ernie put on his jacket to leave, he would take his blunt index finger and press it gently against the end of her perky nose. Usually after that, he didn't say anything else as he let himself out the front door.

Sometimes Beth leaned her forehead against the closed door until she heard him pull the car door shut and start the motor. Other times she'd lean her back against the door, with her eyes closed, waiting for the sound of the car door and then the engine beginning its purr. A few times, she even went to the front window in the living room and pulled back the center of the sheers just enough to watch him depart.

One evening, Beth invited Ernie over to watch a football game between the first and fourth ranked collegiate teams in the country. She knew that ordinarily Ernie would have watched the game with some of his buddies. So in a way, she was kind of testing the depth of his interest in her. When she'd called and made the suggestion, he'd said sure and asked what time, without the slightest hesitation.

At halftime, Ernie crooked his finger at her, motioning her to leave her beloved chair and come join him on the sofa. She was a bit hesitant. He had his arm draped conveniently across the back of the sofa. So she came over and perched on the edge of the sofa with him, pretending to listen to the halftime chatter. After a little while, he moved his arm from the top of the sofa and told her she could lean back now. She did so, feeling rather foolish.

Finally, he said, "Do you think I would be sitting here if this wasn't where I wanted to be?"

"I thought maybe you were regretting not getting together with the guys."

"What I'm regretting is not getting together with you."

Beth wasn't sure how to take that comment, and Ernie realized it had not sounded the way he had intended. As a matter of fact, it had sounded downright suggestive. He reached over to the remote control and, pressing the mute button, turned toward Beth.

"I'd like to withdraw that last comment. It did not come out the way I meant. All I was trying to say is that I wouldn't mind getting to know you a little better, like maybe putting my arm around you or giving you a hug or holding your hand sometimes."

He sounds lonely, too, Beth thought. "Do you ever think of your ex-wife?"

"My ex-wife!" Ernie exclaimed, feeling like he'd been blind-sided. He wanted to ask what brought that up, but Beth wasn't through.

"I thought maybe you still saw her sometimes."

"No chance."

"I mean sometimes divorced couples even remarry."

Ernie stared at Beth, incredulity radiating from his face. She wouldn't look at him. He was too intimidating.

"Beth." She still wouldn't look at him. "Beth," he said again, with more urgency. She turned toward him but kept her eyes lowered, picking at something invisible on the sofa. He slid down and twisted his head enough to catch her eye. That made her giggle. At least that was progress. As he resumed a more normal position, he was able to maintain eye contact with her and stated firmly, "My ex-wife is out of my life, okay?"

"What was her name?"

Ernie leaned his head back, closed his eyes, and exhaled in exasperation. "Her name was Monique."

Beth said nothing, thinking that it was a beautiful name.

He lifted his head and opened his eyes to look at Beth. "What is this? Has someone been telling you some kind of stories or something? Because if they have, it's gotta be lies!" The volume of his voice had risen vehemently.

Beth hadn't meant to stir him up so. Was that an indication that he really was still in love with Monique, she wondered? They were silent for several minutes. Even though the second half of the football game had started, neither one of them pressed the mute button back on.

Finally, Ernie spoke. "I don't like to talk about this, Beth, because it was the biggest mistake I ever made in my life. But I certainly don't want this coming between us. So here goes."

Beth flung her fingers across his lips to stop him, but he just removed them with one broad hand and held them warmly against his chest. "She wanted everything to be perfect. She made me think I was perfect for her. I had just received my law enforcement degree from the University of Missouri. She was only a sophomore. But her folks had lots of good old St. Louis brewery money and didn't think it was important for her to graduate. She could just pick out whatever guy she wanted and tell her parents she'd found him. I was the lucky one.

"We got married. Then, after our honeymoon cruise, she told me that in order to keep everything perfect, she would not even consider having children until she was thirty or older, and maybe never. That in itself might not have been the end of the world. But the way she'd carried on around other people's babies before we got married, and all her talk about who our children would look like, made me feel like I'd been misled, to say the least.

I finally figured out that all her insistence on perfection was really just her means of getting her own way and not being willing to try to reach a compromise on anything. Whenever she felt so inclined, she'd call in her parents to back up her self-centered position. This so-called marriage lasted less than two years."

Beth squeezed his hand, not knowing what to say.

"She is out of my life. Period."

Beth couldn't help herself. She had to ask. "Does she still live in St. Louis?" She braced herself for an outburst of exasperation and frustration on Ernie's part. But he didn't seem to mind the question.

"She went to Southern California not long after the divorce, and her folks bought a place of their own in Palm Springs. Someone told me she got married out there. I sure feel sorry for that poor sucker. Who knows, maybe she married someone as self-centered as herself and they get on famously." He looked at Beth. "I couldn't even tell you which town she's in. All I know is she made my life hell, and now she's out of it forever and ever. Amen! That's why I refuse to drink a certain brand of St. Louis beer. End of story."

Beth hadn't even known about the certain brand of beer. But she was getting to know him better. She'd also noticed that he didn't mention his ex-wife's name again after Beth had asked him what her name was. She reached over and pushed the mute button.

Beth grabbed up the remote. She didn't want him to miss the final minutes of the game. Then she turned around and gave him a big bear hug, which caught him off guard and left him tingling. She was settling back to watch the game before he'd had time to respond. He thought, I'll get her back later, when she isn't expecting it. Man, this sure beats hanging out with the guys again! The game was close, ending with a victorious field goal as time ran out, preceded by a couple of spectacular plays that would run on the highlight reels for a week.

Without warning, Ernie gave Beth a bear hug, which she responded to, returning it instantly. She was used to them, so it would be hard to catch her off guard. Before releasing her, Ernie spoke softly into her ear, "It's a good thing you turned the remote back on. If I had missed the finish of that game, tomorrow the guys at work would have picked up on it, and I would have been mighty hard put to convince them that I just became too deeply engrossed in a conversation to notice how the game was going." Beth began to giggle. "You see, they all knew I was coming over here tonight. They would've drawn their own conclusions, and I never would've heard the end of it." Ernie discovered that a giggling bear hug is even better.

After saying goodnight in the hallway with one last hearty bear hug, arms wrapped tightly around each other, Ernie touched the tip of her nose lightly and let himself out.

On the way home, Ernie held a debate with himself about maybe just making the bear hug a substitute for the nose touch, but finally talked himself out of it, realizing that he'd better continue just touching the tip of her nose. Good night bear hugs on a regular basis could quickly become more complicated.

Chapter 33

BETH INVITED ERNIE to spend Thanksgiving Day with her family. Daughter Linda and her husband Ken, flew in from New Jersey for the holiday and weekend. They brought with them the special news that Linda was expecting late in May.

So Thanksgiving was a joyous and festive day. Ken seemed comfortable with Ernie. They enjoyed watching the football games together. And Ernie soaked up the unexpected pleasure he got from being around Linda, because of all the ways in which she reminded him of her mother.

On Friday after Thanksgiving, Linda finally managed to get some time alone with Nan when the two sisters went off to do some mysterious Christmas shopping.

"Isn't Ernie the greatest?" Nan asked her sister as she started up the deep green minivan and they sped away toward Crestwood Plaza.

"I'm glad you brought up that subject."

"Subject? You think of Ernie as a subject?"

"He seems really nice, Nan. But you've got to remember that I just met this guy. I know that everything you've written to me about him seems to be true. And I understand how he's the one who stayed on Dad's case and that he's been great to both you and Mom. But in spite of everything that you told me, about him being younger than Mom and all, I still wasn't prepared for seeing them . . . together."

"That might have been true, even if he was Mom's age or older," Nan pointed out.

"I guess, but it's just everything about him, his looks—"

"What's the matter with his looks?" Nan snapped, as she slowed for a stoplight.

"Nothing! Absolute nothing! That's what I mean. His looks are fine."

Still waiting on the red light, Nan frowned at her sister, not comprehending her problem.

Linda shrugged her dainty shoulders and admitted, "I'm not sure what I mean. I guess I just didn't expect him to be everything that he seems to be. It's like he's too good to be true."

Nan smiled at that and said with confidence, "You'll see." Then the light changed to green, but she still glanced both ways before entering the intersection.

Tentatively, Linda asked, "Do you think they might be serious?"

"I hope so," Nan said quickly. Then she added more thoughtfully, "I don't know for sure. You know it's been over two years, and Mom still wears her wedding ring."

"I noticed that."

"But you know how older people are today, as unpredictable as young people."

"I hope not! Do you care to expound on that?" Linda asked.

"I'm just saying there aren't many taboos these days."

"You sound older than Mom!"

"I just hope Ernie and Mom stay together," Nan said softly.

ThreadBare

"Why is that so important?"

"Because of all the eligible men among Mom's friends, none of them hold a candle to Ernie."

"Silly girl. You sound like you're in love with him yourself!"

"It isn't that," Nan replied calmly. "It's just that he reminds me so much more of Dad than anyone else does."

"He doesn't look a thing like Dad!"

"I don't mean that way! I mean his character traits are like Dad's. Just recall all the different things I've told you about Ernie. Think of that in terms of what Dad stood for. Then I believe you'll see what I'm getting at."

They were silent the rest of the way to the shopping center.

As they searched for a parking spot in the crowded lot, Linda asked, "Do you think they're sleeping together?"

"No! Just like I know Mom and Dad didn't sleep together before they were married."

"Oh, so Mom told you about that, too."

"Yes. They didn't lose their heads then. And Mom's sure not about to lose her head now." Nan eased the minivan to a stop in a parking space.

"Well, that's a relief!" Linda burst out laughing. "Isn't it difficult raising mothers properly these days?"

As they got out of the car, Nan responded with warm laughter of her own. It was fun to have her big sister back, even if it was just for a little while.

Chapter 34

THE SECOND WEEKEND in December, the law firm Phil had worked for was having its annual party at the home of John Templeton, one of the senior partners. His wife, Vivian, was not only a gracious hostess but also a genuine human being, except for her fluffy blonde wig and thick, dark eyelashes. The Templetons had hosted the Christmas party ever since he had been named a senior partner, twenty-two years ago.

Beth and Phil had enjoyed nineteen of the parties. Beth missed the twentieth one, right after Phil died. But she had gone last year, with a dear friend, a widower for the past four years, from her church. He was at least twelve years older than she and understood that she needed someone kind to be with that evening. He was honored to escort her.

This year she struggled with the idea of having Ernie accompany her to this posh shindig. The men in Phil's firm had been there for her when she needed them so much during those first few months after her husband's death. Most of them had been pallbearers or honorary pallbearers at Phil's funeral. Occasionally, one or another still called to check on her and share family news. These men were invaluable consultants for almost any financial or other legal matter she had to deal with. They were also powerful and influential in the St. Louis area.

When the invitation arrived, she felt it was important that she be in attendance again this year. She thought of taking someone instead of Ernie, but couldn't think of anyone else that she would enjoy being with. Moreover, she couldn't imagine trying to explain her actions to Ernie if she did go with someone else, so she finally asked if he'd go with her. She explained to him as best she could the history and significance of this annual event, knowing it might be quite boring for him.

He agreed to take her, commenting that he figured he was good for at least six hours but warning her that after two o'clock in the morning he might turn into a pumpkin.

Beth realized the evening would be expensive for Ernie when he discussed with her where the best place to rent a tuxedo might be. She wasn't much help, because Phil had owned two, one white and the other black, with tails. So he didn't ever use rentals.

But she checked with a couple of church friends, and they each gave the same shop a high recommendation. She had told Ernie about it, and he'd seemed pleased with the service there. He could have asked some of his buddies for tuxedo advice but didn't want to explain why he needed a tux and then take the ribbing he knew he'd never hear the end of.

Beth regretted that Nan wasn't home to see Ernie when he arrived in his all black tux. Nan even could have taken snapshots of the party couple before they left. She smiled to herself, remembering the times Phil, the proud father, had taken pictures of their daughters and nervous dates before some of the big dances and parties. She must have been a little nervous herself tonight, because when she saw Ernie drive up, she impulsively decided to go ahead and slip into her long, silver-beaded coat instead of waiting for him to assist her.

She was glad she hadn't bought a new gown. It was always hard to tell if it would still be comfortable after being worn for several hours. As for her hair, she always wore it quite short. So she just fluffed it some with the blow-dryer when she finished shampooing it. Maybe that way she wouldn't look quite so much like an impish pixie.

Ernie's red Cougar was glistening on the outside and spotless inside. Ernie had parked it by the small walk that led out to the driveway. She could not remember him ever parking anywhere except on the street in front of her house. It was such a minor but thoughtful and gentlemanly thing to do. But it also made her feel that his parking in the driveway was just another tiny speck of the mortar that seemed to be cementing their relationship.

More specks of mortar were added when Ernie started leaning over to kiss her cheek every time they had to wait for a stoplight. She wondered what he'd do if she ever turned to face him. Probably kiss her nose. But she didn't test him. However, she did regret when they turned away from the stoplights and onto the interstate, heading west toward Chesterfield, through a light flurry of snow.

Chapter 35

WHEN A VALET opened the door for Beth in the Templetons' circular driveway, the sporty red Cougar held its own against the impressive surroundings. Ernie raised his eyebrows ever so slightly as he came around the front of the car and offered his arm. Then they went up the steps of the immense. white-columned entrance to the red brick mansion.

Its 14-foot high, green double doors boasted welcoming live evergreen wreaths, woven with red velvet, which ended in enormous bows. A butler opened the door as they reached the top step and was waiting to take their coats, or in this case, Beth's silver-beaded coat. Ernie did not have a formal overcoat.

Beth removed her black kid gloves, trimmed with black velvet, and slipped them into her coat pocket. Then she almost took Ernie's breath away as she slipped her shoulders out of the wrap, moving her small black-beaded clutch purse from one hand to the other. He handed the heavy coat to the butler, without taking his eyes off her as she turned toward him. She was wearing a long-sleeved white blouse of the finest, translucent cotton cloth, with a trim Mandarin collar of black satin. (Ernie didn't know that's what the collar was called. He would have described it as kind of a mini-turtle neck, with a rounded opening on either side at her throat.)

Underneath the blouse was a silver lame garment. Ernie would have described it as a strapless tube top, except that it had three little straps as thin as spaghetti over each shoulder. He'd never seen her in anything formal before. She really was petite. The collar and the matching wide, black cuffs of the blouse were accented with clusters of pearls the same as those in her dainty, dangling silver earrings.

From a black satin sash, lined with white satin and knotted on the left side, her black, narrowly pleated skirt of crepe followed the gentle curvature between her waist and hips and then flowed straight to meet the pointed tips of her black suede sling pumps. (She liked dancing in those, because they were comfortable.) Actually, the only new item she was wearing was a pair of sheer black hose.

She smiled at Ernie and took his arm again. She knew she was with the most handsome man at the party. It did not occur to her that he was also the youngest. The Templetons greeted them enthusiastically. Vivian reminded Beth of an older and more gaunt version of Miss Piggy. She was decked out in an overabundance of eyelashes, expensive and glittery jewelry and an outfit of hot pink chiffon, with flowing sleeves, flowing pant legs, and four-inch heels to match.

Vivian was still eight inches shorter than John Templeton, who at six feet, six inches, had played basketball and tennis at UCLA. He had a paunch so mild that most of the other men were envious. His tux was black, except for a red and green plaid cummerbund. His face was distinguished in a craggy sort of way. His amber eyes twinkled at Beth from behind rimless glasses.

Beth was surprised at the amount of silver that was

beginning to glint in John's thick, wavy brown hair, which he parted just slightly off-center. Above the mantle of the white marble fireplace in their gigantic living room was a wedding portrait of John and Vivian. They were a stunning couple when they were first married, way back sometime in the sixties.

After numerous necessary introductions made in various rooms and hallways of the ostentatious house, Ernie coaxed Beth to the dance floor. The music, from a live band, was slow and gentle. Here was a refuge from the other partygoers that also allowed the two of them to be physically close for longer stretches of time than they ever had been before.

Beth discovered that as she danced on her toes, like she always did, she could just barely see over Ernie's broad shoulder. With Phil, she had always had to keep her head turned aside if she was to avoid getting lipstick on his tux and if she was to see anything but the studs on his tux shirt. This was going to be different. Ernie had a good feel for the music and led her easily. She was pleasantly surprised to discover this hidden talent. It made her wonder what he must have been like as a teenager.

They danced four slow dances without taking a break. But then their refuge was interrupted by one of the white-haired, senior partners, who was approaching seventy years of age. He tapped Ernie formally on the shoulder, and Ernie relinquished Beth with a good-natured smile. Now he could admire her from a distance. He didn't understand why it thrilled him when he caught glimpses of her pale heels peeking through the sheer black hosiery from the hemline of her dark skirt as she danced, but it did.

As Beth stole glances at Ernie, she felt like she was in a movie with Cary Grant. After all, Ernie had that same penetrating expression, although Ernie's eyes were darker. He had a wonderful sense of humor. And he carried himself with the kind of aplomb that had seen the movie star through so many awkward or dangerous situations. She'd have to tell him about this amusing comparison someday . . . someday.

Chapter 36

AFTER THAT FIRST shoulder tap, Ernie and Beth never seemed to get more than halfway through a dance before someone else was tapping Ernie's shoulder. His good-natured smile began to wear a bit thin. It seems the old man had started something. Ernie was not interested in dancing with any of the other women. However, he did make an exception for his hostess, Vivian Templeton. He was pleasantly surprised at how gracefully she moved on the dance floor, although he felt uncomfortably conspicuous as if he were squiring a pink flamingo around the floor.

After enjoying a pleasant sit-down dinner together with three other couples at a round table where they had found their names on place cards, Beth excused herself to go to the restroom before the dessert was served.

It was almost 9:30, plenty of time for more dancing. This time, she had suggested to Ernie that if anyone cut in more than once, at a decent interval, say 15 seconds, he should cut back in again. She was sure Ernie's solid presence would make any protester refrain from challenging his actions.

"How am I supposed to keep track?" he inquired, intrigued by her idea.

"I know," she replied, coming up with an inspiration. "If

it's a repeat offender, I'll lay two of my fingers in kind of a little V along the back of the guy's shoulder. But instead of victory, it will stand for damsel in distress." How could he resist her?

Beth put on some soft-hued lipstick and left the gigantic bathroom, more like a spa and dressing suite. It would take her half an hour to describe the place to Ernie while they danced. Maybe she'd just urge him to check it out for himself. She was smiling to herself as she started to make her way back toward the band music, past several rooms and passages to other parts of the house.

Then she spied John Templeton standing at the open door of the formal music room, which contained a harp that Beth knew the Templetons did not play. It was strictly for show. There were also a couple of violins on the wall, encased in domed glass and beautifully framed. Near the harp stood a baby grand piano, a lovely dark instrument. John smiled at her and invited her into the room, softly pushing the door closed without latching it behind him.

"You still play the piano, don't you, Beth?"

"No, not me. You may be remembering one of my daughters, who played a couple of songs when our whole family visited you and Vivian one summer day a few years ago."

"Those were good times, weren't they, my dear?" he said warmly, taking her dainty black purse and laying it on a small marble table. Then he took both her hands in his and led her to a settee of royal purple brocade. He sat down and drew her down beside him, still holding her hands. It was easier to talk with him sitting down than standing, where she had to tip her head far back just to see his face. He was, however, still holding her hands.

When she tried to withdraw them, he merely enclosed

ThreadBare

them completely with his own large hands and would not release them.

He leaned close to her, looking into her eyes. His voice was low, as he began to speak. "That's quite a young buck you've got with you tonight, Beth."

She thought to herself, spare me the lecture, and rose quickly to her feet, trying to disengage her hands. He let them go, standing up and sweeping a long arm around her waist to pull her toward him, whispering, "If that's what you're looking for, you should have let me know a long time ago."

He lifted her chin and started to kiss her. She realized this was not going to be an innocent holiday kiss and turned her face aside, trying to shove herself away from him, to no avail. He was strong. He clinched her waist tightly to him. While she pushed vainly against his chest, he bent his head to kiss her cheek, her ear, and then her neck. She was too mortified to call for help, but continued to struggle against his behavior. He was way out of line! She felt her hand score a glancing blow across his face, knocking his glasses askew on his forehead before they dropped to the carpet.

He released her suddenly, and she stepped back to regain her balance. Taking her firmly by the shoulders, he drove her down against the settee. With one of his knees jammed into the cushion beside her and his arms pinning her across her collarbone, he cradled her face in both his hands. Laughing with delight, he said, "You are one exciting woman, Beth Vincent!"

She tried to twist away from him, but still laughing, he held her head and kissed her full on the mouth. She gritted her teeth and flailed at his head and his back. Then she grabbed his hair, trying desperately to pull back his head. She could scarcely breathe.

When he finally came up for air, he grinned at her, his

amber eyes glowing. She slapped him across the face as hard as she could. He pinned her tighter against the settee with his arms, while tightening his grip on her head. "You're a real tiger!" he said, smiling at her maddeningly, and bending his face toward hers again.

"That's enough!" The low voice sizzled with authority. It was Ernie, standing in the now open doorway, holding his clenched fists stiffly at his sides. His eyes were blazing at John.

Templeton lifted his arms from Beth, slid his knee off the settee, and rose to his full, imposing height. Beth leaped up from the settee. But Templeton spoke her name and caught at her arm as she fled, ripping a cluster of pearls from the black satin cuff of her blouse and sending it rolling across the carpet. Still she made good her escape to Ernie's side.

Beth wondered how long Ernie had been standing there. How much had he seen? Her face was burning with humiliation. She felt reddened from head to toe, not as much from the total exertion expended as from a sense of overwhelming embarrassment.

Templeton shrugged with a little smile and commented that he didn't see what all the to-do was about. After all, it was his party, and he was just trying to be an attentive host.

Ernie kept his gaze on Templeton and said in minced tones, "Beth, are you ready to leave here?"

"Yes," she replied quickly, and stepped out of the charming music room, trying to pull herself together. She needed Ernie to hold her in his reassuring arms. But he had not followed her. She glanced inside. Ernie was picking up the cluster of pearls from under the piano bench, daring Templeton to make a move while his back was turned.

John just picked up his glasses and, putting them on, said lamely, "I guess I misinterpreted what Beth wanted from me." Ernie retrieved Beth's purse from the table. Then, at the doorway, he turned and responded to Templeton, pointing an accusing finger at the tall, dejected man. "You should know Beth well enough after all these years to know what she wants and deserves is a man of integrity and decency."

Ernie accompanied Beth as they went to get Beth's coat. Then he handed the purse to her and went to locate Vivian Templeton and explain that Beth was not feeling well. As soon as the words were out of his mouth, Vivian rushed to Beth, exclaiming that she didn't look well. She placed a cool palm alongside Beth's cheek and said, "I think you may be feverish, child." She bade them goodbye as they thanked her for a lovely evening. Before she closed the door behind them, Vivian called out, "You take care of yourself, dear. I'll give you a call tomorrow."

Beth wanted Ernie to carry her down the stairs, put her in the car, take her home, tuck her in, keep her soft bedside lamp turned on, sit by her bed, and hold her hand until she fell asleep.

After the valet brought the car, and they had driven out of sight of the lovely mansion, Ernie turned the radio music off and tried to explain himself. "I couldn't do anything, Beth. I'm a cop. Oh, I wanted to pop him a couple of times! Oh man, I wanted so badly for him to take a swing at me or try to jump me." He emphasized his feelings by jabbing the padded dashboard a couple of times. Beth had never seen Ernie in this state. She shivered and wished the whole evening had never happened, not even the fabulous dancing in Ernie's arms.

"I didn't expect you to beat him up or arrest him or anything. I thought he was going to give me a lecture about getting involved with a younger man."

Ernie was calming down. He heard the phrase, involved

with a younger man, and wondered if it was her phrase or if Templeton had used it. He hoped it was her phrase, that she felt they were becoming involved.

Beth continued. "I was overjoyed to hear the sound of your voice and to know you were rescuing me."

"Hey, I didn't even see a damsel in distress sign from you," Ernie said, looking at her with a teasing grin.

But Beth had missed seeing his playful expression and bowed her head. Tremulously, she asked, "Do you really think I was leading him on? That I liked what was happening?"

Ernie didn't even answer, because he knew whatever answer he gave would not be adequate. As soon as he could safely do so, he pulled the Cougar to a stop on the broad shoulder of the interstate and eased both of his arms around her, which was a bit awkward with a floor shift in between them. He let her nestle her head against his comforting shoulder until the catches in her breathing eased away.

The earlier snow flurries had vanished, and a full moon was peeking through the front windshield, but its charm was lost on the couple inside. Finally Beth straightened herself and told Ernie that she was okay. Then he guided the Cougar back onto its homeward way.

Once they were inside her front door, he took her coat and laid it across the arm of the sofa. Then he came back to her and enfolded her in his arms again. He had thought of several funny things to say, which might make her smile. But he didn't dare share any of them. She was hurting too much already.

Finally, after another long, gentle embrace, he took her hands in his, turned them palm side up, bent his head, and kissed each one of them tenderly. Then he took something from his tux pocket and pressed it into her hand. It was the cluster of pearls. She almost smiled at that.

He gazed at her for a moment with eyes as black as she had ever seen them. Then he stepped back, pressed his index finger ever so tenderly against the tip of her nose, and let himself out, closing the door tightly behind him.

She pulled back the sheers on the living room window just as the Cougar was pulling away from the curb. She watched until the glowing taillights disappeared completely. And then she cried and cried. For Phil, her loving husband. For Linda and Nan, her dear daughters. And because she was so alone. She prayed a lot that night for strength to endure.

Chapter 37

ERNIE CALLED BETH every day during the morning and offered to come by sometime or to take her somewhere. He couldn't even talk her into trying country line dancing, or any other kind of dancing. She kept begging off, saying she had so much to take care of before the Christmas holidays. He wondered is she was suffering from depression. He worried about her and vowed to keep making his routine call each day, listening for telltale signs that she might be slipping into serious trouble.

Then one day, she stunned him with the news that she and Nan were going to fly back to New Jersey and stay with Linda and Ken over the holidays. Actually Beth would be staying for three weeks. Nan would be flying home sooner to take a course between semesters. He thought about offering to take them to Lambert Airport and to pick them up from their return flights. But he didn't. His relationship with Beth seemed to have slammed into a brick wall, and he didn't think a rodeo or anything else was going to make any difference this time.

He volunteered to work a lot of holiday shifts for his colleagues. It made him feel good to know that doing so enabled them to spend precious time with their families. It also helped him keep his mind on the job instead of on Beth.

More than once it occurred to him that he could get himself wounded or even killed if he let his thoughts dwell on Beth too much, especially at a crucial moment. His instincts told him he couldn't afford to get careless. But his heart was asking him why it should make any difference anyway.

In mid-January, on Martin Luther King Day, Ernie again volunteered to work for a buddy on the force. When his phone rang, he automatically said, "Johnson here."

"Is this the REAL Capt. Johnson?"

Ernie recognized Beth's light-hearted voice. He wished his heart could feel the same way. "Do you need something?" he asked bluntly, while he mentally kicked himself hard. "Are you still in New Jersey?" he hastened to ask, trying to sound more civil.

"No, I got back in last night. Of course, Nan's been back at school for more than a week, but she picked me up at Lambert and decided to sleep over last night and tonight, since there are no classes today because of the holiday."

"I guess Linda and Ken are doing okay."

"Oh, they're doing great. And Linda is feeling wonderful, in spite of her pregnancy. They said to tell you hello."

Ernie didn't know what to say. "It's nice you're back." That sounded awfully flat.

"Nan says she wants to pop some popcorn and watch the video of "South Pacific" tonight. We thought you might like to join us."

These Vincent women were going to be the death of him yet. Then why didn't Nan call instead of you, he wanted to bark at her, but he just tightened his lips into a thin line. Unconsciously, he was also clenching his jaw.

"Ernie? Are you still there?"

ThreadBare

"What time?" he asked without enthusiasm, trying to think of a cute little excuse, like he had too much after-the-holidays shopping to do.

"Is seven o'clock okay?"

"Sure."

"Do you have a cold or something? You don't sound right."

Maybe you've just been away from me so long you don't remember how I sound, he wanted to shout at her.

"I'm not contagious. See ya later." He hung up. Had he ever told her NO concerning anything she ever wanted? Even just one thing? He couldn't think of a thing. She had the world on a string, and his heart, too. She was just plain spoiled. She had everything in the palm of her hand. He thought of the night he had kissed those dainty palms. His face softened. He remembered the way they had danced that night. And then Templeton . . . . Thinking even further back, he remembered the first night he'd met her, and had told her that her husband was dead. No, she did not have everything she wanted, not by a long shot.

Chief Kinard was on the way out of his office. He stopped and looked at Ernie. "Will you stop daydreaming? You look like a lovesick puppy or a drowning duck. I'm not sure which." Then he stepped close to Ernie's desk and asked softly, "Are you still seeing the Vincent woman?"

"Yes sir. Tonight, as a matter of fact." He tried to keep his voice noncommittal but knew it had brightened considerably.

"She's a mighty fine lady. I just don't understand what she sees in a bloke like you."

"Thanks, Chief. You're such a confidence builder."

Looking Ernie squarely in the eye, the chief retorted, "Since when did your confidence ever need building?"

The chief continued on his way to the restroom, leaving

Ernie in what would have been a lighter frame of mind, except for something he couldn't admit to himself. He was not only nervous about going to the Vincent home, he was also afraid. Then he thought of Nan. It would be so great to have her around. She'd have him laughing in no time.

Chapter 38

THEY WERE REALLY getting into the movie now, and Ernie's muscles were beginning to relax a little, as they soaked up the lush tropical scenery and enjoyed the marvelous tunes and lyrics. They were in the living room, nibbling from their heaping cereal bowls of popcorn. Nan was stretched out on the floor. Beth was enthroned in her favorite chair. And Ernie, thinking this set up would have been ideal if he were out of uniform, had the sofa to himself. Beth and Nan had never gone back to using the family room much, after Phil died.

Then the phone rang. Ernie pressed the mute button on the remote control. Nan dashed to her bedroom to answer the phone and was back a few seconds later, donning a down vest and announcing that Matt and some friends had just called on a cellular phone. They were on their way to pick her up any minute now. No sooner were the words out of her mouth than a horn tooted and she ran to the front hallway, saying that they were all going to Freddie Froghammer's (a popular nightspot with the younger set) and that she'd try to be back around midnight.

"Around midnight?" Ernie queried, raising his eyebrows to Nan like a questioning father. What does 'around' mean?"

"I don't have a class until ten on Tuesdays," Nan pointed out, "so I can leave here by 9:30 tomorrow morning and still have plenty of time. Glad ya came, Ernie. Bye, Mom."

"Who is this Matt kid?" Ernie asked, as the front door slammed shut.

"Matt Wilkerson is a 26-year-old med student doing some kind of a residency at Barnes Hospital."

"How did she meet him?"

"One of her friends, Marie Garland, works at Barnes as part of her pre-med training. She knew Matt and thought Nan should meet him. She introduced them."

"But she's what, barely 20 years old? That's quite an age difference."

"You're telling me!" Beth agreed, getting up, walking over, and pushing Ernie's knee out of the way so she could sit beside him. "When I was 21, I was already married to a 28-year-old attorney." She picked up the remote control and pressed a button. "Are we going to watch this movie or not?" Strains of "There Is Nothing Like a Dame" filled the room.

Meanwhile, she plumped a small yellow velvet pillow rather vigorously and snuggled it against the small of her back, so that her feet could touch the floor. Ernie straightened himself up on the sofa and tried to concentrate on the movie instead of Beth.

A couple of minutes later, Beth looked over at him and said, "Don't you find it odd that Nan so conveniently gets that phone call after she's set this all up?"

Ernie looked at her with a deadpan expression. Then he sat straight up with a look of amazement on his face. "We've been set up! How could you think such a thing about your daughter?"

Beth looked at Ernie skeptically. "Were you in on this?"

"Me! I was tempted to ask you the same question. After

all, I didn't extend the invitation. All I did was accept it. From you, not your daughter!"

"That doesn't mean she didn't set us both up, the little scoot. I'll get her for this."

Then they became immersed in the musical. It really was a good one, with lots of humor and some touching scenes. When the deep-throated Frenchman began to sing "Some Enchanted Evening," Ernie thought of how clever Nan had been to randomly choose this particular movie. "Once you have found her, never let her go." But the line that hit his heart as true as an arrow was, "Then fly to her side, and make her your own. Or else you may live through your life all alone."

Deeply moved emotionally, and flustered, Ernie glanced at Beth and saw tears glistening in her eyes. He put his arm around her and pulled her close, to comfort her. Was she grieving for Phil, he wondered.

Then he found himself staring at her left hand, which lay loosely in her lap. The stunning wedding ring with its beautiful square-cut diamond was not there. He had never known her not to be wearing it. Quickly, he looked at her right hand. He couldn't see it very well, but he could see enough of her palm to know that she was not wearing a ring on any of her fingers.

He tried to turn his attention back to the movie, but he couldn't seem to see it. The screen seemed to be too far away for him to be able to focus.

Beth rested the back of her head against Ernie's shoulder, slipping off her shoes and drawing her feet up on the sofa, to curl herself within his arm. As the movie ended, and Mitzi Gaynor handed the Frenchman the soup ladle, Beth chuckled and then stood up and stretched herself luxuriantly, like a cat.

Ernie made a mental note to ask her to teach him how to do that. He leaned back and did his own tight version of a stretch, straining the cuffs of his navy shirt. Then he looked up into her face.

"Can I get you anything else to drink?" she asked.

"Nope, I better be shoving off."

"Oh, that's right, you have early shift tomorrow, don't you?" He was sure he had heard a note of regret in her voice. He was certain of it.

As Ernie put on his jacket, Beth stood observing him, her hands clasped behind her back, feeling foolish but nevertheless eagerly anticipating the moment when he'd touch the tip of her nose with his finger.

"Question," she stated.

"Shoot," he responded.

"How come you always press your finger against the end of my nose when we say good-bye?"

Ernie felt himself blush, something he rarely did. "You really want to know?" he asked, cocking his dark head slightly, drinking in her beautiful cola eyes, and forgetting to zip up his jacket.

She nodded, her eyes widening as he told her.

"It's like this. When it's time for a guy to leave, he'd better do it right while he's thinking about it. Or it could get to be too complicated. I don't want to do anything I might regret. And as God is my witness, I would never want to do anything you might regret. So when I place my finger against the tip of your nose, I'm telling myself to turn around, make my legs take me to the door, and leave. Period."

Then Beth did something she had never done before. She rose up on her tiptoes, slipping her fingers around the back of his neck underneath his jacket collar. Shivers were working their way up his spine as she spoke into his dark eyes. "Thank you for being my hero."

His arms closed around her, lifting her toes from the floor, as he covered her face with kisses. Then he kissed her lips, at first tentatively and then with increasing intensity. He could feel her returning the energy of his kisses and her arms tightening around his neck. Finally, he took a deep, deep breath, shuddered, and lowered her gently back onto her toes. Her face looked radiant as he stepped back.

He lifted his right hand with the measured discipline he would use to raise a firearm, straightened his index finger, and placed it lightly on the end of her nose. Then he walked slowly backwards toward the door, and still looking at her face, fumbled for the doorknob, opened the door and went out. Before closing the door, however, he slipped his head back inside, gazed at her with those dazzling dark eyes and said, "I love you, dearest."

She whispered, "I love you, too." Then his head disappeared, and he closed the door softly but tightly behind him. He walked to his cruiser with the dignity of a police officer, but all the way, he felt like whooping and hollering and leaping into the air like a kid. Beth flung herself on the sofa, clutched the plump pillow in her arms, and savored his lingering presence.

Later that evening, as Beth lay in bed, she sent off a lengthy prayer of deepest praise and gratitude to the Almighty for creating a wonderful new love to fill her heart and share her life. As she drifted toward sleep, in her hazy thoughts she knew Snoopy had let the pink thread bare Macklin's deadly deed in order to lead her to Ernie. If they ever decided to get a dog, she wanted to name it Snoopy. She was still smiling as she fell asleep.

Chapter 39

LATE THE NEXT afternoon, Ernie called, and then came by the house to see Beth.

"I think it's time I proposed," he announced.

"A toast?" Beth quipped.

"Don't make this more difficult than it already is."

"Okay," she murmured meekly, taking his hand and leading him to the sofa. But she didn't sit down, so he remained standing, too.

She took his hand and gazed up at him. "There are a couple of things worrying me. I think we should talk about them first," she said, her eyes serious and full of pain. Ernie felt that deep ache expanding in his chest like the time she had first come to his office, seeking her husband's tie.

"Yes?" he said, a cold dread spreading through his body. He was good at instincts, and right now his instincts were telling him Beth had something mighty heavy that she was going to lay on his heart.

"I want for us to live somewhere else."

"You mean you want to move away from St. Louis?" he asked, groping to understand and realizing helplessly that he'd move anywhere to be with her.

"Oh, no! Not that. I just want to move out of this place."

"Your house is beautiful!"

"But it's a lot more than we need."

"Well, I think my apartment is a tad small."

"I know that. I mean another house, but not as large as this one. We don't need four and a half baths . . . or a library.

Ernie slipped his right hand gently into hers and shook it. "Agreed."

Now it was time for the other shoe to drop. The cold dread seemed to be drifting slowly around in his circulatory system. Maybe it contained a frozen clot that would find its way to his heart and stop it from beating.

The pain in Beth's eyes was still there. Apparently she had told him her less serious concern first, and left the worst till last. Here comes the biggie.

"You said a couple of things were bothering you. What's the other one?" He braced himself, unconsciously assuming the stance he used on the firing range.

"You indicated that you would like to have had children. I don't think that would be wise for the two of us, unless we considered adoption," she admitted sadly.

He felt weak at the knees with relief. "But I'll have two fantastic daughters, and a fine son-in-law!"

"Yes, but they are grown. That's different."

"Ah, but having a grandchild is the best of all possible worlds, so I'm told. And besides, you know something?" He gazed down at her tenderly as she shook her head. "I'd want to be with you and only you, even if you didn't come with all the extras."

He could see the pain evaporating from her eyes and wished with all his heart that he had been able to put her mind at rest before that pain ever started to take hold.

"Was that enough of a proposal?" He could see a

ThreadBare

twinkle in her eyes now, as she shook her head that it was not enough.

He sat down, patting the sofa beside him in invitation. As she sat down next to him, he put his arm around her and pulled her close. It felt as right as it had last night. He gently turned her chin so he could look straight into her eyes and asked, "Will you marry me; be my wife; and love me the rest of our lives?"

Her voice was strong and clear as she replied, "Only if you will marry me; be my husband; and love me the rest of our lives."

Ernie swallowed a lump in his throat. And he had thought she was the one who would get emotional. Beth threw her arms around his neck and kissed him hard. Then, before he could recover and respond, she wriggled away from him and jumped off the sofa. Looking off into the front hallway, she whispered, "I thought we should seal it with a kiss." Ernie was well aware that this was the first time she had been the one to initiate a kiss.

"When should we tell your daughters?" Ernie asked, reaching out to catch hold of her hand.

Beth stood there, loving him intensely for remembering the girls and trying to think for a moment. "It should be sooner, rather than later."

"I agree," Ernie confirmed. "That is just fine with me," he murmured, drawing in a deep breath.

"So how about going out to get a bite to eat and then coming back and trying to give Nan and Linda a call?"

"Sounds good to me, Beth. Do you realize I can never give you a wedding ring like you had before?"

"Matching wedding bands will be fine. Let's just have special inscriptions engraved in them," she suggested, smiling tenderly down at him. Ernie didn't know if her mind was working fast or if she'd been giving this some thought for a long time. Wow! She was one interesting woman!

Beth waited for Ernie to stand up. Instead, he pulled her back down beside him on the sofa and started kissing her. She hopped up again and pulled him, groaning, to his feet.

Chapter 40

EATING BURRITOS AND tacos at a local fast-food haven, Ernie and Beth sensed that for the first time nothing stood between them—no suspicions, no misunderstandings, no shadow of a fine tax attorney, no ex-wife, no more guessing games.

Beth wiped her mouth with a paper napkin and said, "I have an ulterior motive for moving." Ernie's eyebrows rose. "I'm banking on the people in a new neighborhood not to realize much difference in our ages."

"I won't tell," Ernie mumbled, licking a drop of ketchup from his thumb.

"Since you're getting a few hints of silver along the edge of your sideburns, people may think you're older than I am!" Beth's eyes were twinkling.

"Do you think I should start dyeing my hair?"

Coming from Ernie, that comment made Beth laugh out loud. "Absolutely not!"

"Do you know what the chief's reaction was this morning when I walked into his office? Even before I said a word, he said, 'You're getting serious about that Vincent woman, aren't you?' He could tell just by looking at me!"

"What did you say?"

"I said, 'Yes, sir, you hit the nail on the head.'" Then he asked me what I intended to do about it. I just smiled and told him I'd keep him posted, and that I hoped to have an update for him in a day or two. Then, the rest of the day, whenever he caught my eye, he'd grin those big teeth of his from ear to ear."

When they returned from eating, they tried Nan first, turning on the speaker of the phone in the living room. They reached a female voice, but it wasn't Nan. She said, "Just a sec." Then they heard her say, "Nan! Your folks are on the phone."

Before Nan picked up the phone, Ernie quipped, "It sounds like her roommate already has us pegged!"

Nan listened intently to what her mother and Ernie were telling her. Then she was ecstatic, saying she knew it was inevitable, but chided them for taking so long. "When's the wedding?"

Beth and Ernie looked at each other. Then Beth explained that they hadn't set a date yet.

"Why not have it in April? That's a beautiful time of the year, and it's still two months before Linda's baby is due."

"Actually, we're considering sooner than April," Ernie heard himself respond, while Beth looked at him with an expression of astonishment on her face.

"Who are you inviting? All of St. Louis?"

This time Beth spoke. "I think it will just be a family wedding at the church," she glanced at Ernie, "with a few close friends, perhaps."

"That'll be cool. Just let me know, and I'll be there. Oh, except this Saturday's out. I have a heavy date, both afternoon and evening."

"Who with?" Ernie countered.

"Matt. You remember him? Matt Wilkerson. He came by and picked me up when you were at the house."

"The only thing I met was the tooting your mother and I heard as you dashed out the door. Remember?"

"That's right. It's too bad you didn't get to meet him. He's a swell guy."

"And I've been meaning to talk to you about that quick exit that evening, young lady."

"Me too," Beth chimed in.

"Hey, I gotta go."

"Wait," Ernie insisted. "I want to know what you're going to be doing with this swell guy all day on Saturday."

"Well, dad-to-be, first we're going to see the new space exhibit at the Science Center. Matt hasn't had a day off in eons, and he's dying to see the exhibit. Then we'll eat somewhere in the Central West End and go to the free jazz concert at Wash U. He has to be back at the hospital by ten P.M. Is that a sufficient account?"

Ernie realized he'd been a bit heavy-handed. "I'd like to meet him sometime. Maybe we can work around his schedule so that he can make it on the day I marry your mom."

"I love hearing you say that." Her comment made Ernie smile, thinking Nan really must be kind of serious about this med student. But she continued, "That part about you marrying Mom. I just knew it!" She would never cease to amaze him, Ernie mused.

Having seen Beth's look of astonishment while they were talking to Nan about a date for their wedding, Ernie suggested they at least select a couple of weekends before they called Linda and Ken, to make sure one of those dates would work okay for them. Beth agreed, but pointed out that there would have to be enough time to make preparations.

"How much preparation is needed for a small family wedding, Beth?"

"I have to look at a calendar," she retorted.

He produced one from his billfold, and she studied it very carefully. "Well, since Saturday is out, how about the first or second weekend in February?" She returned the calendar, but Ernie didn't even recall putting it away.

"Ernie? Do you have a problem with that? It's just that sometimes doctors don't let their mothers-to-be do any flying in the final few months of pregnancy."

He looked at her with merriment in his dark eyes. "I don't have a problem with either of those weekends. With a supreme effort, I should be able to get all my preparations and details taken care of in time."

She snatched up a newspaper and started rolling it. His eyes widened in mock, and he ducked into the kitchen to hide. Then he caught her by the waist as she burst through the doorway and persuaded her to surrender her threatening baton in return for his bribe of a sweet, lingering kiss.

Made in the USA
Lexington, KY
07 January 2017